Young Razzle

by JOHN R. TUNIS

YOUNG RAZZLE

WILLIAM   MORROW   &   COMPANY

NEW YORK

PUBLISHER'S NOTE: On baseball teams before 1950, unlike those of today, it was not unusual for the team's manager to also play one of the positions in the field. In this book, Spike Russell is both the Dodgers' manager and its shortstop.

Young Razzle

CHAPTER ONE

THE old lady sat in the rocking chair fanning herself. Without looking at her, Joe realized her disapproval. Yet he went on packing with care. Spikes. Flannel shirt. Underwear. Socks. Stockings. Sweater. Cap. Glove. He checked every item.

All the while, even though he couldn't see her, he could feel her attitude. It was in the air, in the quick squeaking of the rocker. Whenever Grandma was upset, she rocked like that, the noise betraying her emotion.

At last she couldn't keep still. "I set in this same chair and watched your pa pack his valise to go to the depot, same's you're doing. I told him no good would come of it. He took no notice of me, same's you, Joe."

For almost the first time in his life Joe found him-

self sympathizing with his father. Why should anyone want to stay in Waycross? What was there in
Waycross anyhow? What chance had a boy got in
this place? And now that his mother was gone, what
was there to hold him? Nothing.

The old lady continued to talk while he rolled up
a clean undershirt and tucked it into a corner of the
suitcase. He was tired of the argument that had now
been going on night and day for a week, ever since
the man had stopped off to ask him to report to the
baseball club. "Look, Grandma, you want I should
stay here and work in the freight yards all my life,
or drive a truck for Cassidy and Spears?"

"We went through all this with your pa. He was
stubborn, same's you. I tell you, Joe, sure's you're
born, no good'll come of it."

My father, my father, my father! I wish to heaven
she'd leave him out of it. Why does she keep throwing him up at me? What's he got to do with me?
Nothing. Never has had.

Joe leaned over the suitcase, a frown on his thin
face, checking the contents once more to be sure.
The socks were fresh and clean, so were the stockings that went over them, so also was the flannel
shirt. He realized how his grandmother hated to see
him leave, now that his mother was dead, and most
of all how she disliked to see him going into base-

ball. But if he was to go, he was certainly going with clean clothes. Grandma had seen to that. She had washed and ironed everything herself, not trusting them to Fanny who usually did them for him. It was, in fact, when he discovered Grandma washing his second pair of socks that he realized she had finally accepted the inevitable.

"Your mother was set against it, dead set against it. She never would have allowed you to go if she was here, son. She knew this baseball; she knew what it does to a man. She had a-plenty of it when she was young. She saw what happened to your father. He just took off and left her flat. Baseball made a no-account man out of him. It'll do the same to you."

"No, Grandma, no . . ."

"No wonder she hated baseball. It broke up her home and it really killed her. But for baseball, she wouldn't have been left alone to run this big boardinghouse, and it was this place that finished her. Once your pa got into baseball, he clean forgot everyone to home. He left your ma to shift for herself. You'll be the same way, selfish and no-account."

My father, my father again! Always my father! "Please leave him out, Grandma. I ain't Pa. He ain't got nothing to do with me. When a fella gets a chance like this . . . once in a lifetime a fella gets a chance like this."

"Your ma would never have let you go, never." The old lady shook her head, rocking back and forth. Yet in her heart she knew this was untrue. He would go, just as her own son had gone years ago in spite of her pleading, and not even her daughter-in-law, had she been alive, could have stopped him. Two years ago, yes. A year ago, perhaps. But now Joe was seventeen going on eighteen, finished with high school, older and determined. There was the same stubborn look about his mouth and chin that she had seen on her own son years before in this same room. "No good'll come of it. You wait and see. No good'll come of it," she murmured half to herself, for by this time words were too late. Words might have stopped him the year before when his mother was alive; not now. Nevertheless she felt she still ought to use every argument. "We both hoped, your grandpa and I, that after your ma's death like that you'd stay to home and help us round the house."

Joe straightened up, tall, thin, tanned. She was so old, so feeble, so delicate to run the big boarding-house that his mother had completely managed for years. But yet, he couldn't miss a chance like this. How could he explain to her what it meant? Either you were hauling wood for Fanny, the elderly cook, hustling suitcases for the railroad men who dropped off for a night's lodging, doing odd jobs, cutting the lawn, running errands. Or . . . playing second base for High Point. And then . . . well, who knows after that?

How could anyone compare it? How could anyone hesitate when such an opportunity came? You'd be a fool if you didn't take it. The High Point scout had asked you to sign up. He came to you. No one could possibly turn down a chance like that.

The old lady, thin, worn, her blue eyes shining under her white hair, gripped the arms of the rocker so intensely that the whole chair squeaked louder than ever. Joe noticed it and went over to her, taking her bony hand in his big brown paw. For a second or two, as he looked down at her, she looked up at him, appeal in the blue eyes. It made him feel guilty to walk out, to go away leaving the two old folks trying to carry on alone. And yet, and all . . .

Nugent, No. 54, second base, batting . . .

"Look, Grandma, you wouldn't want I should give up this chance, would ya? Would ya now? It's my only chance, and I'm pretty darn lucky I had this one. If that scout hadn't of seen me playing last Labor Day against that team from the Railroad Y, and if I hadn't had a good afternoon, I'd never got it, never. See now, this is only the start. I'll go on from High Point. I'll be sending you back money every week, regular-like, you wait and see. Why, if I make good, I'll pull down forty maybe fifty bucks a week. Might get the job of driving the bus that the team travels on. I drove the school bus last year. That's twenty, twenty-five more."

Joe felt his grandmother's protest coming. Her fingers gripped his hand with a strange intensity for one so old. She shook her head, so he went on quickly, before she could speak. "Yep, I know all that. I know what you're going to say—my pa never sent money home. How many times do I hafta tell ya . . . I ain't my old man. Soon's I'm a regular on some good team, soon's I get out of a Class D club, you'll be getting that money order every week, wait and see. Pretty soon you and Gramp won't have to run this-here boardinghouse no more. You'll be free and easy, see? Understand?"

The door opened and an old man entered, tall like the boy, but stooped. The woman in the rocker paid no attention to him and spoke, still looking up at the boy.

"No good'll come of it. We went all through this with your pa, right in this same room here. You'd never be allowed to go, never, if your ma was here to stop you. She'd rather see you dead than in that-there uniform. She had enough of baseball, a-plenty of it in her lifetime, poor girl."

The old man stood listening, looking at the pair by the rocker, at the suitcase on the bed, packed and ready. "Now, Mother, now, Mother, that's no way to send the boy off."

"I'm not sending him off! He's going!" she said fiercely. Her fingers gripped Joe's so firmly he couldn't disengage his hand.

"Sure and all, but you want the boy to hang around here all his life, Mother? Come on, son, it's almost time."

The grip of the old lady's fingers tightened still more. Joe leaned down and kissed her. It was necessary to pull his hand out of hers, so tightly did she hold it. He walked across the room and shut the lid of the small suitcase, painted to look like leather. One clasp had broken, so he tied a piece of clothes-line around it and cut the rope with his pocket knife. Then he strapped his bat to the handle.

"G'by, Grandma. Don't take on now. You'll be hearing from me soon."

She nodded, managed to smile, a twisted, dismal sort of smile. But she said nothing; indeed there was nothing more to say. He went out, down the hall, and into the street with the old man.

Two blocks from the house he saw Mr. Matthews, the president of the bank, coming toward them. With a sinking feeling Joe realized there was no escape, for one look at the suitcase with the bat strapped to its side would tell him everything. He came nearer, saw them, and a grin came over his face.

"Well, son, well, you're really off, aren't you! I saw in the newspaper where you had an offer from . . . from some team . . ."

"Yessir. High Point in the North Carolina State League. 'Course it's only a Class D club, but a fella has to start somewhere."

His grandfather spoke up. "He can't miss. They all tell me the same thing, he's a natural like his dad. He can't miss."

"Aw now, Gramp, I ain't even got there yet. They're probably five-six boys trying out for my position."

"Well, I sure wish you luck, son, I sure do. Of course now, your father there, he went up right fast. He's a big-leaguer now."

"Yessir," Joe said quickly and added to his grandfather, "We gotta make that bus, Gramp."

They turned into a side street, for Joe wanted no more conversations with friends or friends of the family, with that inevitable reference to his father.

Everyone always had to drag in his old man. They walked along, saying nothing for a couple of blocks. At last his grandfather spoke.

"Funny thing, it was a spring day just like this one when I walked down this same street with yer pa." Here it comes, Joe thought, my father, my father again. "We was goin' to the old Central of Georgia depot in those days, 'stead o' the bus station. Seems like yesterday. I'd taken him to see the Reds play an exhibition game with the Dodgers two years before, and he was a Dodger fan right from that moment. I bet before that game was over he had the autograph of every man on that ball club. He only had one ambition from then on—to play ball for the Dodgers. He sure has done it, too. He's pitched for 'em eight seasons now. Won more'n a hundred games. I bet anyone knows anything about baseball knows Raz Nugent. Y'know, son, I took yer pa to his first game of baseball. You, too, re-member?"

Joe remembered. It was his first year in high school, and the old man told him to come home from school after recess and he'd fix it with the teacher, but not to say anything to his mother or grandmother. He remembered how the two of them sneaked into the park, and the rain came down in the sixth. He had been afraid the game would be called off, but the Dodgers and Yanks battled until the fourteenth. Joe remembered also what his mother said when they came back late for dinner and she found they had been to a baseball game. Some things you couldn't forget.

Bus Station. A big sign loomed up around the next corner, so they turned toward the place. It was small, dirty, crowded. There was a line at the ticket window and Joe had to wait quite a while. "Ticket for High Point, please." Change at Augusta. Change at Columbia. Change at Charlotte.

Now that he was actually going, leaving home, he began to be worried. There was a funny feeling in his stomach, the feeling that now, at last, he was on his own. An empty feeling, that's what it was.

"Augusta, Washington, all points north, track two!"

The old man took the suitcase and shoved through the crowd ahead as though he wanted him to leave. Perhaps he wanted to get the parting over; perhaps twice in his long life was too much.

There was the big blue bus with the illuminated sign in front—*Washington*. Tomorrow this bus would roll into the Union Bus Station in Washington, and he would be out on a diamond in High Point, and Gramp would be back there on Summer Street, hauling wood for Fanny, doing the errands.

"Good-by now, son. Take care of yerself. And write yer grandma. Whatever you do, write her."

Joe grasped his grandfather's thin and bony hand. Then he picked up the suitcase and turned suddenly, smacking a lady with the end of his bat and almost knocking her over.

"Beg yer pardon, lady, beg yer pardon."

"Why'n you look whatcha doin', young man?"

Joe climbed into the bus and stowed his bag away. Gramp nodded cheerfully, waved, and then walked off into the station. He wasn't waiting for the bus to leave.

CHAPTER TWO

EVERYTHING about Joe Nugent made the fans think of his father—the cocky way he walked across the diamond, the easy, confident stance at the plate. Joe's quick tug on the visor of his cap was identical with the nervous gesture his father always made whenever things got tight in a game. Joe tried hard to rid himself of these mannerisms, and succeeded save for the last one. And whenever he did it, whenever there was that nervous tug, the older fans in the park would invariably turn to their neighbors. "There! See that? Just like old Razzle, isn't it?"

Some of the men on the High Point team started to tease Joe about it, to call him Young Razzle, and kid him about some of the less amusing peculiarities of his parent in the big time. At first he paid no attention, usually walking away as though he didn't hear them.

Then one evening when he was worn down and tired from rides in the jolting bus and frequent night games on poor diamonds under insufficient lights, someone called him that name once too often.

He turned quickly. "My name's Joe! Joe Nugent . . . understand? Get it?" There was such fury in his words, such intensity and anger on his countenance, that the other player stepped back, astonished. Then realizing quickly that his teasing had struck home, he naturally continued to hammer away in a bantering tone.

"Say! Seems like if my pa was a real big-leaguer, seems if my old man was a regular starter on the Dodgers, I betcha if they called me Young Razzle I'd be mighty pleased."

"Cut that out! You heard me now." Joe came closer, still furious. One or two players passing balls paused to watch, here and there a head turned, several men in a pepper game stopped.

"Yessir, if my old man was Raz Nugent of the Dodgers, believe me, fella, I'd feel mighty good when the gang called me Young Razzle. Why, believe me . . ."

He never finished that sentence. Joe suddenly reached out, grabbed a bat from the hand of a nearby player, and rushed at his tormentor. There was a businesslike look in that swinging club, and the other man, realizing the boy was aroused and dangerous, didn't hestitate. He turned and ran for his life.

Round and round they ran until, when they passed the bench, the manager and two of the coaches stepped out and caught the irate youngster. The bat was wrenched from his hand.

"What the devil you mean, going for a guy like that, Nugent? You want to kill my best pitcher?"

Joe stood there panting, hands on his hips, glaring across where the other man had retreated to safety.

"I will, I sure will if he keeps calling me by that name."

"You listen to me," said the manager. "You quit this fighting and take it out on the other clubs, not your own teammates, see? Now get in there and have your raps."

Sportswriters in the different towns where they played soon discovered that he was always civil and agreeable when addressed as Joe. But if they called him Young Razzle or mentioned him in a news story by that name, he took pains to ignore them.

At first Joe had many troubles. It was difficult to be the son of a big-leaguer, especially a man who was still competing and was in the daily papers every morning. Each time the club played a new town the fans were critical. They expected a lot and were often disappointed if he failed to star. But after a while this was forgotten. He became a person on his own—Joe Nugent, the kid that's burning up the base paths around second for High Point.

The lights in the night games bothered him greatly and for a while his timing was way off. Finally old George Dixon, the manager, took him in hand, changed his stance slightly at the plate, and showed him how to meet the ball. His batting picked up. But playing at night was new to him, and often the lights left much to be desired. In one town, nobody was sure on long flies whether or not an outfielder had caught the ball until he was running back with it in his glove. Not even then, at times.

They were playing a night game in Winston-Salem one hot evening. A runner on first tried to steal second, and the throw from the catcher hit the man on the foot. The ball bounced high into the air and vanished in the semidarkness. Joe instantly whirled, twisted around, searching for it. So did the shortstop, backing him up; so did the center fielder, charging in to cover up. The runner, seeing the three fielders looking frantically for the ball, dashed for third, and went on to score the winning run before Joe discovered it out on the grass behind the shortstop's position.

The next time they played the same town Joe was ready for revenge. His chance came when the same man came up at a critical moment of a tie game. With a man on second base, he struck a slow, bounding roller to his right. Joe fumbled the ball momentarily, turned, picked it up and threw. The throw was wild and over the first baseman's head. The runner rounded first and headed for second, where Joe calmly met him with the ball and tagged him out.

What had he thrown past first? A potato, taken from his pocket, so the other side claimed.

Instantly the umpire was surrounded by a vociferating throng. He was out! He threw a potato! He did not! He did so! You can't do that. Why not? The umpire questioned Joe closely. Was that a potato you threw?

Joe was innocence itself. "Why, sir, where would I ever get such a thing as a potato?"

The debate continued at length, and when the other manager demanded that Joe be thrown out of the game, George Dixon asked under what rule he could be excluded. The umpire was perplexed. Finally in disgust he turned away from the wrangling mob and ordered the game to continue. The man was out and the game was eventually won by

High Point. The story went all over the circuit, and everyone agreed it was a trick worthy of Joe's father at his best. Raz had always been a famous practical joker.

By the end of Joe's first fortnight with High Point, he had won his job as a regular at second base, and by the end of the first month his hitting was so improved that he was up with the leading sluggers of the team. In July, Dixon moved him into the clean-up spot.

The diamonds on which they played ranged from fair to terrible. There were fields that were bad enough in the daytime and positively dangerous at night. Every few days the boys would pack themselves into the weary old bus and jounce over the mountain roads. Hickory, tomorrow; Winston-Salem, Friday; Rocky Mount, Saturday. One night they would play at home, a contest that was seldom finished before midnight. Early the next morning they would be off in the bus for a town anywhere from one hundred to two hundred miles away.

Moreover, on their five-dollar-a-day travel allowance, it was necessary to eat and sleep in the cheapest places—tourist courts, motels, boardinghouses. Often when they were scheduled for a night game and arrived in a town in the afternoon, the boys would not check into a hotel at all because they couldn't afford any such luxury. They simply wandered around for several hours until dinnertime, and then walked out to the ball park. There Joe would climb into his dirty, stiff, sweat-stained road uniform, and take the field under the indifferent lights to try to play ball. When the game was finished, he took a hasty shower in the dingy dressing quarters under the wooden stands, with the rats running in plain view along the pipes, and, when dressed, climbed back into the bus again to leave town at midnight.

For this punishment, and the punishment was visible in his tired face, in his weary movements in the last innings of a game, he received a salary of $37.50 a week. Out of this he found himself, even with their travel allowance added, having the greatest difficulty in getting a place to sleep and enough to eat. Not to mention that fifteen dollars he sent home every week. Somehow he always dug that fifteen dollars out, but the others began to think of him as a tightwad.

"Now there's a young man who appreciates what a dollar will do," remarked one of the old-timers on the club, watching Joe waiting to read a newspaper someone was finishing in a hotel lobby. Even the job of driving the bus, which he had hoped to get because he had driven the school bus at home, was staked down by the star pitcher. He would often drive them two hundred miles at night and then take the mound against the league leaders the following evening.

The poor lights, the insufficient food, the jolting, swaying bus rides after long games in the torrid heat of midsummer, all this was new to Joe. There were many times he felt sure he wouldn't be able to stand erect after a hard game, that he would simply have to turn in his suit the next day.

It was toward the end of the season that he first got hints of a reprieve. High Point was in second place in the North Carolina State League and was fighting madly for the lead. One night George Dixon was standing beside the bus talking to a reporter from a local newspaper. The bus was supposed to be air-conditioned and the windows kept closed; but the air conditioning had long since broken down and never been fixed. So the windows were open. Naturally the early comers got the window seats, and Joe, seated in one of them, heard the voice of his manager. One sentence made him sit up.

"Well, how ya expect me to win with a team of cripples, hey? Don has a bad back. Jack has a bum arm—so he says. Tonight Jess comes down with the flu and we have to leave him here in the hospital.

Red swung a bat at Rocky Mount the other night and pulled a clavicle or something. How many's that? Four . . . five? O.K., four. Arthur Stein has a bad hip; ten days at least for him. That Italian kid who was supposed to pitch me into a pennant got a bad Charley horse. Jake had to go North to his father's funeral. Then this evening I get the clincher. Oh, this is really the pay-off. The boss tells me Savannah in the Sally League is after this boy Nugent, willing to pay big dough, too. Will he let him go? *Will* he! That guy would sell his mother if there was enough cash in the deal!"

CHAPTER THREE

THE rest of the nation was enduring a heat wave. Not Boston. In Boston that particular afternoon was cool, windy, threatening rain, with a strong northeast wind. It was a game both the Dodgers and the Braves needed, a game Spike Russell, the Dodger manager, especially wanted to win. He had called on Raz Nugent, his only pitcher who was rested and reasonably likely to defeat the Braves.

Raz liked to pitch in Boston where there was space for the outfielders to catch long drives that might be home runs in other parks. The big hurler was, therefore, full of confidence that dismal day.

By the sixth inning, the Dodgers had presented Raz with a 5-1 lead, a lead that should have been sufficient to let him win in a walk. Ordinarily he would have maintained that lead easily. Unfortunately, the heavens opened up about this time, and a slow, persistent drizzle began to descend. Raz, who depended not on speed but control, who always liked to fool the batters by clipping the corners, knew that a wet baseball would probably mean trouble for him. He glanced with dismay at the sullen, lowering skies, turned, and tossed the ball over to Spike Russell at short, and walked slowly toward Stubblebeard, the umpire behind the plate. Stubble understood perfectly before Raz spoke. Without a word he motioned him back to the box with a wave of his hand.

Grumbling and scuffing the dirt which was now turning to mud, Raz obeyed. As he had feared, his control went off. He gave a couple of bases on balls and by the time there was one man out, the Braves had scored two runs to make the game closer. Once again Razzle walked in to protest to the umpire. He was an impressive figure, stamping in with both hands extended, looking up at the glowering heavens and shaking his head at the drizzle which was now sweeping in gusts across the field behind that northeast wind. Obviously if the game were called, the Dodgers would win, 5-1. This would make Raz's record look better, a fact he knew perfectly well.

On the other hand, the Boston team realized that Razzle was getting annoyed and upset, and they felt victory was highly possible if the game continued. The fans yelled and yowled at Razzle. Even the hardy group huddled together under newspapers in the bleachers jeered as he walked in once more to the plate, shaking his head, arguing, protesting, complaining at conditions overhead and underfoot. And also taking time while the rain came down.

But Stubblebeard was immovable. "Get back there, Raz! Play ball," he said shortly, looking at his watch, for he realized like everyone that Raz was stalling, hoping a real deluge would descend any moment. The Boston manager, who had jumped from the bench to make his own protest if the game was stopped, returned to the shelter of the dugout. Raz, slapping his soggy thighs, trudged back to the mound.

The game continued and so did the rain. After the sixth the storm increased somewhat, and the three umpires, Stubblebeard behind the plate and the two men on the bases, held a short conference. Their desire was to prevent a protest from the Braves, because double-headers were piling up toward the end of the season, so the announcement was made that at least one more inning would be finished, if possible. Like most umpires' decisions, this was not received with pleasure by either side.

However, the Braves' pitcher went quickly to

work, burning the ball in and hurrying play as much as possible, while the Dodgers stalled to the limit in hopes the deluge would force the umpires to call the game. Slowly, one by one, the three Brooklyn batters went down, and it was time for the Dodgers to take the field. Obviously this would be the final inning and the Braves' last chance to win.

They raced in, eager for their raps, while the Dodgers took the field more soberly. Only the mound was empty. Stubble turned with annoyance toward the Brooklyn bench. At last Raz appeared at the entrance to the lockers, and emerged from the dugout. He was an amazing figure. On his head was a Gloucester fisherman's rubber hat which came well down over his ears. Over his shoulders hung a floppy raincoat, the collar turned up, and he carried an umbrella which he opened as he waddled toward the mound.

The fans were delighted. Raz Nugent, that's old Razzle for you! They rocked with laughter and greeted him with impartial cheers. Unfortunately, Stubblebeard failed to see the humor of the situation.

He yanked off his mask in annoyance as the crowd's guffaws reached his ears and Raz, dressed in an outfit that would have been suitable for an Indian monsoon, came forward. The umpire's face was grim, his lips set. He took several steps to meet the big Brooklyn pitcher.

"Razzle! Quit that horsing! Stop that clowning and play ball or I'll chuck you out of the game. Now get that rig off and go out there and pitch!"

Raz stopped, an injured expression on what Stubble could see of his features. "No sir, no sir, no *sir*, Stubble. By golly, I'm not taking no chances. I got me a real bad cold over in Philly last week, and if I take these off, likely I'll catch pneumonia."

"Take 'em off, Raz!" The jeers and cheers of the crowd grew louder. They were of course unable to hear the colloquy between umpire and pitcher, but they saw plainly that the former's authority was being disputed. Being against all umpires on general principles, they liked it. There stood the man in blue, his hands on his hips, snarling at Raz, while under the opened umbrella was the big Brooklyn pitcher, an innocent look on his face.

"For the last time, take those rags off!"

"And get pneumonia? No, thanks. If I do, Stubble, if I get pneumonia, I'll sue you and the league for a thousand bucks."

Spike Russell had stood enough. He came rapidly across from deep short, exasperation on his face and in his quick steps. It was bad enough to blow a sure lead in an important contest. But this was by no means the first time Razzle's clowning had cost the club a game, and he was annoyed and aroused.

"Hey look, Showboat, cut this out. That's about enough horsing round. Now get yourself out of those clothes and play ball. Understand?"

Raz shook his head slowly. "No, Spike, not me. No sir. Not in no storm like this, I ain't pitching. Old Raz ain't no sailor, he's a ballplayer." With that he stepped across to the equally irritated umpire and, taking the old man's arm, pulled him under the dripping umbrella. "Come on in out of the rain, Stubble. What's the sense of getting all wet in this storm?"

Now the noise from the stands had a different tone. The joke had lasted long enough. With the increasing drizzle, the crowd was anxious for the Braves to bat before the real northeaster, plainly on its way, developed. They knew that in the rain Razzle's effectiveness was diminished. In the rain he was apt to be wilder than a Texas steer. So the noise rose from the stands. It was directed both at the pitcher and the umpire.

Immediately Stubble realized his authority was being flouted brazenly before the crowd. It was enough. One arm extended majestically toward the bench and the dugout and the showers under the stands, and warmth and clean, dry clothes. No words. No comment. None were necessary. His meaning was plain to everyone.

Grumbling and mumbling about the injustices of society and baseball umpires in particular, Raz turned and shuffled toward the bench. His umbrella went down. He stepped inside. The noise from above followed him until he disappeared from sight in the recesses of the dugout.

The Brooklyn bull pen had paused to follow the unusual show, watching Razzle's antics with joy. Unfortunately they had become chilled and none of the pitchers was really well warmed up when Spike Russell gave one man the signal to come in. He took the box and was promptly shelled by the Braves, who drove in three runs and won the contest, 6-5. The damp, disgusted Dodgers trooped in silence from the field, their uniforms soggy, their shoes soaked, water pouring off their caps and down their shoulders.

Half an hour later most of the boys had cleared out, but Spike Russell sat in the manager's room talking with Charlie Draper, one of his coaches. Spike always hated to lose, and he hated especially to lose a game that was already won like this. His tone was evidence of his annoyance.

"That cowboy! That clown! Why, we had the

thing wrapped up and paid for, Chuck. Then Raz has to get funny."

"Enough's enough," remarked Charlie sagely, leaning against the wall and lighting a cigar.

"Boy, you said it. I'm sick and tired of paying a man twelve five to be a showboat. Time's gone when he could be depended upon to win fifteen games a season, year in, year out. He's through; he's washed up. He thinks now he's Olsen and Johnson, got to be gagging all the time. I tell you, I'm sick of it."

"No use talking, he ain't winning no fifteen games nowadays."

"Shoot, I didn't mind the time he tried to catch a fly with one hand behind his back. I didn't mind the time he hit the foul pop and ran after the catcher astride his bat like it was a hobbyhorse, yelling and shrieking. Remember? I didn't even object in that game when Stubble was giving those close ones to the Cubs, that game last month . . ."

"When he took his shirt off and told Stubble to wear it and play on our side for a change. The old man never forgave him for that one. He was right though, Raz was right. Stubble had it coming to him."

"I know, I know. I didn't fine him. I didn't say anything much. But this is the limit, this losing a game we needed, one we had in the bag. Shucks, I guess I've got to get rid of the guy somehow. He's no good to us."

Charlie took the cigar from his mouth. He looked at it critically. "Spike, I got an idea. Marvin Mason in Montreal needs pitchers badly. You want to get that young Chase, that outfielder of theirs, and have a look at him. Mason has all the fly catchers he can use. He'd jump to get a shot at Razzle. He knows Raz would be hot in their circuit, might even pitch him into the play-offs. Why don't you send the old Showboat up there and let Mason struggle with him?"

Spike was silent. He turned it over in his mind, hating to part with a man who had been around the club when he came up, for whom he had affection. It was difficult, yet it had to be done. Besides, he knew Mason would be pleased to have Razzle on his staff.

"Charlie, y'know I believe you have something there, I really do. We're not going to win a pennant this season; not with old Raz Nugent, anyhow. He's too fat, he won't train, he's out of condition. Maybe a shake-up would do him good, rock him so he'd go up there and take off some weight. If he did, if he got into shape, we might even bring him back again . . ."

"As a bull pen pitcher, as a reliefer."

"And I'd like to have that boy Chase down here these last few weeks and get a good look at him. Fact is, this afternoon was the pay-off. I determined some time ago the next time he got to showboating, I'd let him out. I warned him, too. Those boots! That umbrella! It's too much. I just can't take him any more. Suppose I call Mason after dinner and get his O.K. Tell Harrison . . . have Harrison make out a ticket for Raz to go up on the night train . . ."

"He could get to Montreal in a couple of hours by plane tomorrow morning, Spike."

"Nope, he won't travel by plane. Shoot him up tonight."

"You want to see him yourself? You want to tell him or have Harrison do it?"

"Let Harrison do it. Shucks, I'm sorry to see him go, at that. Well, he brought it on himself. Have Harrison fix it up."

CHAPTER FOUR

RAZZLE, now a minor leaguer and not enjoying it after being a star pitcher and somewhat of a prima donna for ten seasons in the majors, started the following year on the Montreal Royals. Their training was not done in the usual luxurious surroundings in Florida to which he was accustomed, but in a small North Carolina town during a cold and windy March. During much of the month little play was possible. Consequently Raz got off to a bad start and was in trouble from the beginning. Unlike the youngsters who found it easy to limber up, to bring soft muscles into condition, his aging arm and even more timeworn legs refused to respond quickly in the chilly spring windstorms.

On the Dodgers Razzle had been among friends, men with whom he had much in common. They

had gone through long campaigns together. He
knew them and liked them and they liked him. He
had played under a young manager who had come
up to the club as a rookie from Nashville; they respected each other as players, and Spike Russell
had known how to handle the temperamental hurler.
With Montreal, on the other hand, he was among
strangers, and under a manager who regarded him
this second season as somewhat of an expensive
luxury. Even though his pay had been almost cut
in half, it still remained a top salary for a club like
the Royals. Mason, the Montreal pilot, expected re-
sults for his money. He did not conceal this fact
from Raz as the season advanced.

The spring and early summer in Montreal were
really cold that year. This retarded Raz and pre-
vented him from rounding into form, for he was
above everything a hot weather pitcher. In game
after game he found himself tight and unable to
get his control. More than once he started only to
be knocked from the mound within a few innings.
This was a new and humiliating experience. Never
before had he been unable to hold his end up on a
team.

His first good game was in late June against the
Orioles in Baltimore. It was a hot Sunday, a really
hot day at last, the kind of an afternoon Razzle

reveled in. This, he thought as he went to the park, is my weather. So he took an unusually long rub-down before going out, and went into his warm-ups slowly and with care. He was determined to come through with a well-pitched game, and his arm felt easier and more limber the longer he threw. The fans began yelling at him from the moment he went out to join his catcher, anxious, in that peculiarly sadistic way of baseball fans, to ride a vulnerable player. Raz, of course, affected not to hear them, and in between pitches he conversed with a sports-writer from the *Sunpapers* who was standing watching.

"Understand your boy is burning things up down there with Savannah, Raz," said the reporter, mak-ing conversation. In the International League, as in the majors, Raz was known by sportswriters over the circuit as always good for a story with a new angle. Friendly, agreeable, he was never reticent, and was a favorite with newspapermen if not with the fans.

"Yes sir, he sure is," said Raz, pausing. He stood a minute slapping the ball from one hand to the other. "I tell ya, Bud . . ." To Razzle all sports-writers save the few attached to the Dodgers, whom he knew well and called by their first names, were Bud. "I tell ya now, he really is. They hasn't been a second baseman in the Sally League since I can remember like that youngster. Only one season with a Class D club, then whang! Savannah picks him up for five thousand dollars and last summer he batted .360 for them. He'll top that by ten points this year, wait and see."

Before the reporter could answer, Marvin Mason, the manager, passed by on his way to the bench. His face had a worried look, the look of most pilots of pennant winners who wake up one morning and find themselves in the second division. He was anxious and short of temper and, seeing Razzle standing in conversation, he exploded.

"C'mon, Raz, c'mon, big boy! C'mon now, tune up that old flipper of yours. Don't just stand there horsing round all day."

Mason moved along toward the dugout with quick, nervous steps, leaving Razzle, hands on hips, surveying his back with no enthusiasm. Raz had seldom been addressed that way in the majors and he didn't like it.

"Who does he think he is anyhow? Yeah, and who does he think I am? Just one of the hired hands, I s'pose." Muttering these words to himself, he then turned to the reporter. "Drop in after the game, Bud, will ya? I'd like to show you the clippings I got on the boy. Oh, yeah, I take the Savannah papers every day. Say, you're gonna hear a lot more about that kid soon. He's a Class A leaguer now, but you mark my words, you take it from old Razzle, he won't stay there long. No siree."

With that pronouncement he turned back to his chores and the reporter moved off.

Slightly annoyed, Raz took the mound half an hour later. The sun, the heat, and the looseness of his arm at last made him the Razzle Nugent of old. The Oriole batters could not take pitching like this. They were confused by his change of pace. They stood and stared as his hook caught the corners in a tantalizing manner. The Royals took an early lead and held it. This was particularly annoying to the local fans, who thought of Raz as a washout, an old-timer, a man on his way down and out. One of the most insistent tormentors, a man with a cowbell and a raucous voice, was on him all through the contest, making no secret of one of the big chap's better-known weaknesses, and insulting him with taunts that Raz had heard in other towns and other ball parks before.

"Have a beer, Razzle, have a beer, old-timer." It was an insult to which he was accustomed, and Raz shrugged it off without difficulty. But his effectiveness that day irritated the sparse crowd, and the stands began to take up the refrain as inning after inning went past and the pitcher kept complete command of the situation.

Probably all would have gone well and nothing would have happened if Raz had received decent support. But on that afternoon when for the first time in the year he reached his best shape, the men behind him fell off. In the seventh the shortstop let an easy roller go through his legs; the center fielder misjudged a liner, which went past for three bases; a high throw of the second baseman to first on an easy chance, followed by a sacrifice and a long fly, brought in three runs and tied the score.

Some pitchers would have taken it as all part of the day's work, but Raz was edgy enough to be upset, and returned to the bench at the end of the inning in a furious mood. He slumped down beside one of the coaches, muttering, "Three runs without a single clean hit! Gee, I don't know is them guys with me or against me."

The local fans rose triumphantly, feeling certain their taunts had contributed to the downfall of the visitors. Accordingly they concentrated upon the luckless Raz, who happened to be at bat that inning. Tired, hot, annoyed, he made the fatal error of replying to the jeers of his persecutor with the cowbell, who was riding him hard. Turning as he left the dugout, Raz called to the stands in a voice that carried, "Aw, yer grandmother's pajamas!"

The fan stood, delighted, ringing his bell with vigor, and when Raz was retired on three pitched balls his frenzy reached its zenith. By this time Razzle had realized his mistake and paid no attention. The Royals were set down in order, and in no good mood he walked out to the mound.

Perhaps it was his annoyance and the consequent loss of concentration which inevitably follows, or perhaps he was tiring. In any case his control suddenly went to pieces. He passed two men, gave up a single and a double, and was replaced by a new pitcher. Slowly and reluctantly he came in toward the dugout, hot, tired, disappointed, angry with himself, his team, the fans, and the manager. Most of all he was angry at that exultant customer with the cowbell in the fifth row.

"Have a beer, Raz, have a beer, old-timer," he shrieked, waving his bell. "Ya ain't got it, big boy, ya ain't got it no more. You're finished, you're all washed up, Razzle."

Unfortunately these words struck home. Raz could stand it no longer. Pitching his glove into the dugout, he climbed with considerable agility up the stands and toward the offender. In a minute he had him by the shoulders and, throwing him back on the seat, began to pound his face.

Instantly other players on both teams, fans, special policemen, ushers, and onlookers joined in. A general free-for-all resulted, in which black eyes and bloody noses were exchanged all around by both players and fans. Raz himself was well battered about the face when he was hauled off and shouldered to the safety of the Montreal dressing quarters.

A police escort was necessary to get him out of the ball park and away from the indignant fans. The luckless Raz, with a dressing-down from the manager ringing in his ears, sought consolation in a good meal in one of his favorite restaurants. There he celebrated a sore shoulder and a blackened eye so successfully that when he stumbled back to his hotel after dinner he was relieved and at peace with the world. The events of the afternoon, the probable stiff fine the league management would hand him, were all washed from his consciousness.

In half an hour he was stretched out in comfort on his bed with a newspaper in his hands. He lit a cigarette, glanced over the sports pages, and then threw the paper aside and picked up the Savannah daily which had, on his instructions, been forwarded from Montreal. Rain had washed out an evening game in Savannah, so there was no news from young Joe. He dropped the paper and in a few minutes was fast asleep.

One half hour later he began to be aware of something far away, off in the distance and unconnected with him. Raz stirred uneasily. There was a noise, a hammering, a yelling and pounding somewhere in the next suite or the next room or down the corridor. He came to with a start. He sat up. No, that noise was at his door. He looked around. The room was cloudy with smoke.

He sat dazed for a few seconds before he jumped up. Then a chair beside the bed burst into flames. Smoke poured from it, almost filling the room.

"Hey . . . open up there!"

"Hey, youse, open that door."

"Razzle! Oh, Razzle! Wake up, Raz!"

"Open the door, Raz, open the door."

Half-choked now by the thickening smoke, he stumbled to the door and fumbled sleepily with the lock. At last he managed to turn it and the door swung open with a bang, knocking him back against the side wall. Half a dozen people poured in—firemen with axes and extinguishers in their hands, managers and assistant managers, one or two players, and last of all Marvin Mason, looking frightened as well as furious.

That was the clincher, the last straw. Raz had settled his fate, although he didn't know it at the time. Ten days later he found himself leaving Montreal with a one-way ticket to Toledo, a sixth-place club in the American Association.

CHAPTER FIVE

YOU can't keep 'em down on the farm for long if they have the stuff. Joe Nugent suddenly found himself involved in a complicated deal which ended up with his promotion to a better team in a faster league—Kansas City in the American Association. It was all new and exciting. New faces, new ball parks, new hotels, new methods of play. The Kansas City Blues were a mixture of big-leaguers going down—older men who really knew their stuff, and promising young rookies like himself, every one of them fighting to become a regular. Naturally the major-league teams looked to their farms in the International League, the American Association, and the Pacific Coast League first, so there was always the chance a youngster might, in an emergency, be summoned up overnight. This put added pressure on the younger men every minute.

Perhaps the hardest thing about it for Joe was the fact that he didn't have a regular berth. Nor did he receive any intimation from Grouchy Devine, the Kansas City manager, that one was imminent. First, he was used as a pinch hitter and substitute outfielder, a position he found strange. Then he played a week at third base when old Jake Wilson got a Charley horse. Next came ten days of bench-warming, after which he was thrown into several games to rest Nelly Piper at second base.

There he was in his accustomed spot and felt much happier. However, before he could really find himself, before he got completely used to the veteran Mac Sweeny at short, he was out and back on the bench for a couple of weeks, seeing action only a few times in the next fifteen days and then merely as a pinch hitter. This lack of play hurt his game. His batting eye fell off. No matter how much practice he took in the cage he couldn't get a hit in a game. It worried him, for he knew perfectly well that rookies who don't hit are not carried for very long by any ball club.

But his hitting picked up again and once more he began to feel himself in the running for a berth as a regular. Grouchy, he realized, was watching him carefully, and on several days in succession Joe was put in as a pinch hitter.

It was the ninth inning of a night game against the Indianapolis Indians when Joe was called on to bat for the Kansas City pitcher. No score and no one out. Dale Carson, the Indian pitcher, was fast that evening, and Joe only managed to get a piece of the ball, hitting a slow, lazy-bounding roller toward short. He was annoyed with himself at his failure to connect cleanly, and lit out for first with everything he had, his long legs eating up space. It was a grounder on which most players would have been out by three feet, but Joe's speed enabled him to beat the ball to the bag.

Anxiously he stood watching the bench and old Grouchy, with his cap over his eyes, peering out into the lights of the field. The signal came for a bunt on the second pitch. Jake Wilson, the batter, laid one down almost directly before the plate. The Indians, a hustling ball club, instantly converged upon it from every side.

The first baseman and the third baseman, who had expected a sacrifice, came charging in. The pitcher, ten feet off, came toward it. So did the catcher, throwing away his mask. But the ball hopped, bounced, rolled to the left of the plate, and it was the third baseman who was nearest.

He rushed in, shrieking, "Mine . . . mine . . . I got it . . . I got it!"

His coordination was perfect. Racing ahead, he leaned gracefully down, stabbed the ball with his right hand while running, and threw to the second baseman, who was covering first, all in one motion. It was a well-executed play, a pretty stop and throw. The fans applauded as the runner was out by two feet. But this very drive and hustle cost the Indians dearly.

With everyone concentrating upon the play at first base, Joe Nugent saw his golden chance. The momentum of the third baseman's onrush had carried him well toward the plate. The shortstop was camped on second for a possible force-out. So Joe rounded second and without hesitating raced ahead to the empty sack at third base.

Instantly everyone's attention turned upon him. The first baseman, the second baseman, the fielders, the men on the Indian bench, all saw what was happening and yelled a warning. Too late! Now everybody on the Indianapolis team was back-tracking frantically. It was the pitcher who finally got to third base, taking the throw, only to find that Joe had already slid in safely. There was a runner on third and only one out.

Joe, yanking at his cap, noticed Grouchy turn and

speak to Hank Bowers, the coach, by his side. He knew it meant they were talking about him, commenting upon his quick thinking. Now if only he could score that run. Old reliable Mac Sweeny at the plate hit the first pitch to deep center field, a fly on which Joe easily came home with the first run of the evening.

It seemed as though the whole club, rookies, rivals, everybody, was on the dugout step with hands outstretched in greeting as he came panting toward the bench. It was warming and good to feel their sweaty hands, to have them clap him smartly on the back and hear their words of praise. For almost the first time he felt himself one of the team.

Five minutes later the third man went out and the Kansas City Blues took the field for the last of the ninth. Grouchy leaned down the bench.

"Jim, take over third. Nugent, go in at left, will ya! Bill, get yourself a bath. Hank, give that big lefty out there the sign to get himself ready."

Grouchy, Joe knew, was shifting his club around, putting in his fastest and best defensive players. As he walked out onto the field in the lights, he fully realized the importance of those next three outs. Kansas City was leading the American Association, two games ahead of the Toledo Mudhens, who after a poor start were now in second place. Every game was vitally important.

Then a roar swept suddenly across the stands. Joe glanced up at the scoreboard, and saw that the Brewers had just defeated Toledo, 6-5. If Kansas City won this game, they would be three full games ahead of the Mudhens.

Joe recalled a remark one of the coaches had made that night while they were dressing. "This-here's a club that hits the long ball; make one mistake and they'll have three runs home before you know it." He determined, whatever happened, not to make a mistake. This was his chance, his big chance; this was the moment to capture a regular berth, to prove to Grouchy he really had it. He smacked his glove twice with clenched fist. This was it. Here's the big moment.

Scarcely was there time to register all this when the batter at the plate swung. He met the ball, which soared to left, a hard, low-flying liner just over the shortstop's outstretched glove, a ball impossible to catch, one that was easily good for three bases if it got past Joe into open territory behind him.

Yet Joe went for it. Forgotten was his decision to play safe, to make things sure. He took the bolder course. Instead of waiting to grab the ball on the first bounce, he charged ahead. The stands rose, silent save for a kind of collective "Ah" that came up from the whole field. They stood watching that race between man and ball—the long-legged boy sprinting over the turf, the white sphere sinking fast, faster, faster. Now he neared it. His cap flew off. His glove went out in a last, despairing lunge. That impact of ball in glove could be heard in every corner of the park.

Some players would have dropped it. Not Joe Nugent. Some would have stumbled, tumbled, perhaps come up with it in one hand, perhaps not. Joe was far too sure-footed to fall. His balance perfect, he raced on, straightened up at last, drew back as he slowed down and gunned the ball to the infield. Even the local fans stood cheering him although it meant their last-minute rally was probably nipped at the start.

One down, two to go. The next batter fouled out to the catcher. The Indians had only a single out left and the game seemed almost finished. The fans crowded the aisles and exits. Then, with victory practically in his hip pocket, the pitcher blew up.

He lost the third batter on balls, and the next man, a pinch hitter, smacked a drive down the left-field line which Joe raced for, reached, and fired in to third in time to prevent the runner from first taking an extra sack. That was all for the pitcher.

Grouchy walked out to the mound, and big Lefty James, their stopper, who had pitched only two evenings previously, shuffled across from the bull pen. Now the fans were up. The bleachers ceased their movement toward the exits. A single would mean a tie game, and the winning run was parked on first.

Grouchy Devine was manager and managed the Blues himself with no help from anyone. But he permitted Lefty James, a veteran pitcher, one small peculiarity. Lefty liked to arrange his outfielders for every hitter, and this Grouchy allowed. So, after throwing in his warm-ups, the big left-hander turned and shifted his right fielder back and toward the foul line. He waved his hand, more, more. Then he moved the center fielder toward the right and farther back, and lastly motioned Joe toward center and back also. It had taken minutes to arrange the other two fielders to his satisfaction, and when he got around to left field he was cursory in his instructions. It was evident he expected a ball to be hit toward right center.

But Joe was afraid of a long single dropping in left field. The Indian slugger was at the bat, two men were out, and both men on base would be running on anything. He determined to cut off that single and, if possible, prevent a score. So at Lefty's order he moved well over toward center and back a few steps. Then, the moment the pitcher turned to take his signal, Joe edged in again.

Two minutes later he realized his mistake. It was a terrific clout. He recalled suddenly that ominous sentence of the coach. "Make one mistake, and they'll have three runs before you know it."

Looking up as he ran, he sighted the ball going through the lights into darkness, then slowly descending into the lights far ahead. Directly beyond was the wall. He could have played it safe and taken the ball off the wall. But he realized his error had probably cost the game and, determined to make up for it, deliberately challenged the wall.

He gave a final burst of speed. There was a sudden impulsive clutch, an outstretched arm reaching up. Together they met, ball and body, body and concrete. Joe bounced off the wall with the ball in his glove, the final put-out of the game.

The next day Joe had eaten his dinner alone and was going up to his room in the hotel. He realized what a mistake he had made the night before and he wanted to see no one. The elevator stopped at the third floor and Grouchy entered. The manager glanced casually at the people in the car, saw Joe, and raised his eyebrows.

"Fifth," called Joe.

Grouchy leaned over as he pushed to the front of the car. "Next time, son, next time you better do what the old-timers tell ya, huh?"

Joe nodded, lips tight. The car stopped and he stepped out.

Doggone, he thought as he went down the corridor to his room, doggone that old eagle-eye. He don't miss a thing.

CHAPTER SIX

A SUDDEN silence settled over the stands in Ruppert Stadium in Kansas City.

It was strange, not the usual silence that comes in the tight moments toward the end of a long, close game of baseball. The roar from the crowd had stopped abruptly and for a good reason. The fans were watching to see something unusual, something that seldom happens. A rare event in baseball like a triple play or a no-hit contest. Something that's written up in the papers the next day, something you can remember and savor and talk about for years afterward. Something about which you say, "Oh yes, I was there in the park that day. I saw it happen myself."

Every fan was quiet, watching the bench where Grouchy Devine, the Kansas City manager, was

bending toward a tall boy with a bat in his hand.
It was the last of the fourteenth, Toledo ahead 3-1,
two men aboard and two out, the Mudhens and the
Blues both far ahead of the other teams in the
league, both so close to the pennant they could
smell it.

All at once the silence ended. Everyone began
talking.

"Look! There's a pinch hitter coming up." "Wise
guy, hey! Of course a pinch hitter's coming up, with
the pitcher at bat. But is it him?" "Who's it, anyhow? Nope . . . it isn't . . . yes, it is! It really
is!" "Yep, it's Joe." "There he comes. It's Joe all
right." "Joe's gonna bat against his old man." "Joe's
coming up with that war club to knock the stuffing
outa his pa. Hey, Joe-boy, hey there, Joey, hit one
for me. Hit his fast ball over the fence." "Save us
like ya did yesterday against the Brewers, and last
week when the Saints was in town. Win another for
us, Joe-boy." "You got the old guy's number, Joe.
Knock the old geezer outa there."

For the first time in big-league baseball a father
and son were to meet on the diamond.

The man in the box, hot, tired, panting, watched
the boy come forward. What he really saw was himself twenty years before, fresh, young, confident.
Himself with Grouchy Devine at Davenport in the

Three-Eye League, himself as a youngster, tall, rangy, long-legged, breaking into the big time and loving every minute of it.

The boy standing there in the batter's box had a strained look about his mouth. It was the first time the Nugents had faced each other, the first time they had even seen each other for years. Yet there was no nod of recognition, no glint of greeting in the boy's eyes, nothing but a cold and unfriendly stare as he stood waving his club. Raz on the mound turned away, leaning over to finger the rosin bag so nobody could notice how he felt.

Meanwhile Joe watched him closely. Although he had spotted his father the moment he emerged from the dressing quarters, this was his first look near to. So that's him! That's the great Razzle! Joe was moved and disturbed and shocked at this close-up of what had once been a great man in baseball. This was not the loose, grinning Raz Nugent of the newspaper sports pages. This was not the hero of the World Series, the strong man, the first-string pitcher of the Dodgers. Why, anyone could hit that fat old geezer out there, that figure with his stomach hanging over his belt. Why, he's old, he's paunchy, he's lost his stuff. See, he can't even pick up that rosin bag without grunting. Let me at him,

let me just get one good smack at his fast ball, all
that's left of it.

Joe instantly realized his father's fatigue after the
long afternoon of throwing. This was the moment
for him to make good, before that Sunday crowd.
He knew that more than this crowd were watching,
that fans all across the nation were interested in this
encounter between father and son, that he could
make a name for himself in one fleeting second. No
uncertainty entered his mind as he tapped the plate
and faced the panting figure in the box, standing
with his hands on his hips.

The people in the stands jumped to their feet,
yelling. This was it, this was what they had come
for—the clash between the old Nugent on the way
down and the young Nugent on the way up. Up
from Savannah in the Sally League where he batted
.357 and stole 44 bases, where he was the leading
hitter and knocked in more runs than anyone in the
circuit. Up at last to a Triple-A farm club, the finishing school for major-league prospects. Up with
a reputation of his own, not his father's. Up the
tough way, too.

Joe glanced again at the fumbling figure on the
rubber, watched him yank at the brim of his cap.
He knew instantly that his father was the more
nervous of the two. It gave him added confidence if,

indeed, he needed any. For he was determined to show up this man he had been taught to hate, and he knew he had the stuff with which to do it.

Raz grunted, wound up quickly, and shot in his Sunday pitch. The arm of the umpire went to the right, strike one, and the fans yelled. Joe's bat never left his shoulder. Now he patted the plate confidently with his club, sure of himself, waiting. His spikes scuffed the dirt and he dug in, the coolest person in the park. Once more he looked out toward the big chap towering above him on the mound.

What he saw was reassuring. The pitcher was ahead at the start of their duel, yet Joe knew he was worried, for he stood hitching at his cap, shaking off the catcher, waving the outfielders around to right. Or perhaps it was his condition that made him seem worried. Joe saw the family resemblance in their height and carriage, in the way they both yanked nervously at their cap brims with that quick, nervous gesture. There it ended.

So Joe stared scornfully at an old man, out of condition, thick through the hips where he himself was lean. Sweat fell off the oldster, etched the armpits of his shirt, made a damp spot around the seat of his pants that was plainly visible as he leaned toward the rosin bag on the grass. Even from the plate Joe could hear him huffing and puffing as he glanced back at the runners on the bases and raised his arm to go into his motion. There! There it comes!

Raz threw the ball. It missed the corner by eight inches. One and one. The boy set himself for the next delivery and this, too, was outside. Two and one. Now Raz was behind and in trouble. Joe realized that he was stalling between pitches, taking all the time he could, standing motionless on the slab to catch his breath, to summon up energy for the next one.

That slowness finally affected Joe; he wasn't having any more of it. So he stepped out of the box, backing away, in a perfect furore from the stands behind. Leaning over, he rubbed dirt on his fingers with brisk, easy movements. Then he stepped back in and tapped the plate, thinking, He'll try to cut the corner on this one. I better be ready.

Razzle threw. Ball three!

Instantly the big man, anger on his face, stormed toward the plate, protesting, gesticulating, arguing. Sweat dripped from his face, poured down from his cap, and he was gasping for breath as he drew closer. No one knew better than Razzle Nugent that words from a pitcher never change an umpire's ball-and-strike decision. While Joe stood calmly watching, his bat on the plate, the crowd began to yell raucously. There was a trace of scorn on Joe's lips as the older man, slapping his glove angrily against his thigh, returned to the mound.

For some moments he stood yanking at the brim of his cap with that familiar motion. Then he called time to the umpire and suddenly stalked off the rubber and walked to the bench. Joe knew it was a stall, that he was desperate for time to get his wind, to pull himself together for the big one. He watched unconcernedly as his father stepped inside the dugout, toweled himself with care, then moved across to the water cooler. Why, the crazy fool! Is he going to drink water now, right at this moment? He's crazy. And he calls himself a ballplayer, Joe thought with contempt.

Raz took a long drink, then another. Finally he turned, held out his hand for the towel again, caught it, wiped off his face and hands, his neck and arms with deliberation. At last he emerged from the dugout and walked slowly to the mound. Joe watched. This is it, the three-and-one pitch. The old cripple. Coming from an old cripple, too, he thought to himself.

Without delay, with no extra motion, Razzle wound up and threw. It was at the level of Joe's letters, right where he could crack it, and he did. The moment the ball left his bat he knew it was gone.

Raz knew it, too, the second he heard that hard, clean sound. It was by no means the first homer ever hit off him. Indeed they had been coming frequently of late. But this was different. This one meant something. This had been struck by his own son.

He turned in the box, watching. The ball landed in the confusion of a hundred scrambling fans in the outer bleachers, while the runner scurried around the bases and his boy, or rather himself in Davenport twenty years before, loped past second base. Tall, lean, his strides were wide, even running loosely as he was.

Another picture suddenly came equally clear in Razs mind—the picture of himself fat and out of condition and growing old, the picture of a pitcher who drank too much beer and took too little exercise, the picture of a player who was through with baseball at last. He saw himself hanging up his monkey suit in the clubhouse for the last time. And his own boy had done it, had finished him off, had shown him up before the big crowd and put the clincher on him. But then, you couldn't blame the boy. He had to look out for himself.

Delighted, ecstatic, at the sudden turn of the tide in favor of the home club, the fans watched as Razzle crossed the diamond and came slowly toward the dugout. Joe was rounding third as his father approached the base line. Ahead of him was that paunchy figure with the roll of fat slopping over his belt, sweat running off his ears. Coming down the path at a jog trot, the smack the third-base coach had given him as he passed still smarting his back, Joe saw with surprise an extended arm ahead. His father's hand stuck out toward him.

Brushing it aside with his hip, he jogged along to the plate. "Watch out there, Whale Belly," he said curtly as he went by.

CHAPTER SEVEN

THE telephone rang and rang again. Razzle came to slowly, reached over, fumbled in the dark, hit the instrument several times before he managed to get a grip on the receiver. Finally he found his ear.

" 'Lo," he answered in husky tones.

"Mr. Nugent? Long distance. New York calling." There was a pause and at last another brisk feminine voice on the wire. "Mr. Nugent? Mr. Casey of the *Mail* calling . . . all right, Mr. Casey, I have Mr. Nugent for you."

"Hey there, hey, Raz! That you, Razzle? This is Casey." His voice was firm and strong as usual, for like many sportswriters Casey was most awake in the middle of the night when other folks were usually asleep.

"Yeah . . . lo there, Casey."

"Say, Razzle, the A.P. has a story on the wire that you've been given your unconditional release by Toledo. That right, Raz?"

Razzle tried to pull himself together. So here it is! At last. This is how it happens. After years in the majors, two World Series, and almost a hundred and fifty victories in the big time. The phone rings and some newspaperman in New York tells you that you're through.

"Yeah . . . that's right . . . I guess *so,* Casey." After the events of the previous evening when Rusty Snider, the manager of the Toledo club, had attempted to break up a little party in Razzle's room, he was hardly surprised. Their argument had been violent, ending with Raz throwing his boss headlong into the hall and calling him a small-timer. As he listened to Casey's polite, regretful phrases, he began to wish he had not been quite so positive with Rusty.

"Uh huh. Yeah, thanks. Thanks lots. Well, that's baseball for you," he muttered. "I say that's baseball for you. So long, Case-old-boy; so long, kid . . ."

He fumbled with the receiver in the dark, still not wholly awake. Shoot, that's that. A guy pitches his heart out for a club, drops a fourteen-inning game by a single run, by one run, mind you, loosens

up a little afterward, and bang! He's through. He's
out. He's handed his walking papers and learns of
it first through an A.P. wire.

Shucks, thought Razzle, sitting on the edge of the
bed, his head in his hands. It had to come some
time. Everyone gets to be thirty-nine—if he lives
long enough. And at thirty-nine a guy can't go on
forever, even in the minors. From the pennant winners to the second division, from the second division to the small time in Montreal or Columbus,
from Montreal to Toledo and so on down, until you
find yourself pitching semi-pro ball on week ends
through the tank towns of the South for a few dollars a day.

No, sir, not for me. Not for old Raz. When I'm
through, I'm through. I'm finished for good and all,
and I know it, too.

He switched on the light and yawned, looking
with disgust about the room, at the empty glasses,
the beer bottles on the table, the cigarette stubs
in the ash trays. His mouth was heavy and dry. The
air was stale with the odor of smoke and beer left
in the half-drained glasses when the party had broken up. He glanced at his watch. 4:30 A.M. Fine
time to wake a guy out of a sound sleep and tell
him he's through with baseball.

Well, don't kid yourself. That's how things are.

That's the way they gave it to Ed Harrell who used to manage the Yanks. Some newspaperman, some sportswriter he don't even know, calls and tells him he's out of a job. I'm through just because I happened to let the boy hit my cripple yesterday, because I wanted a little sociability, because I wanted to loosen up after a hard one. It's tough though to get it from a stranger, through an A.P. despatch this way.

Aw, shoot, it had to come. When your own son, a young rookie, starts hitting you for homers, it's about time to quit. No use talking, they aren't locking up the store any more of an afternoon to come out and see old Razzle pitch.

Actually there was some relief in his bitterness, almost a feeling tinged with pleasure as he saw the end of the road. Raz Nugent was no longer young, and he was tired of the pennant grind. You get sick of the everlasting strain, first place, second place, first place, a month to go, two weeks to go, ten days left. You get tired of traveling in old Pullmans and dingy coaches where the air conditioning is invariably breaking down on the hottest days of midsummer. You get sick of restaurant meals cooked at three in the afternoon and kept for hours in steam ovens. Raz wanted rest and good food, not the tasteless stuff they give you in hotels and cafés.

Well, he thought, it had to come. It's kinda good to have the decision made for you, even if it is your own kid who knocks you off. At that, I'll be glad to quit, I believe. I was glad to leave Montreal and I'll be glad to get out of Toledo, too.

He rose. "Raz, old-timer, you're through. Boy, you're finished, you're washed up," he declared to the empty room. "Well, it happens to everyone. Now it's your turn."

His eye fell on an evening newspaper carelessly tossed behind an armchair, open as usual at the sports page. There was the schedule of games—National League, American League, International League, American Association. From force of habit, Raz ran his eye down the list.

"Toledo at Kansas City. Night. (Stone vs. Bottone.)"

I'll never see my name in there again. Never again. I'm through, I'm done. Raz stood motionless, staring at the blank wall in front of him. He did not notice when the newspaper slipped through his fingers and fell to the floor.

CHAPTER EIGHT

Unlike many pilots in the minors who were often big-leaguers breaking into a new job and taking it out on the youngsters under them by learning on the job, Grouchy Devine had been around as a manager for a long time. Consequently he had seen lots of ballplayers come and go; but this boy presented a new problem. Whenever a difficulty like this arose, Grouchy would light a cigar and sit alone in the dark, wrestling with it until he found the answer. This was how Joe Nugent found him early that evening after the game.

"Come in, come on in, Joe." Grouchy leaned over and switched on a table lamp at his side. "Come in and set down. I wanted to talk things over with you." What he saw was a tall youngster, just over six feet, with the kind of wavy hair that makes women want to run their hands through it. It made Grouchy think of the way Raz's hair had looked years before.

"How's things working out, Joe?"

The boy was not quite comfortable as he sat in the stiff chair facing his manager. He inspected his finger tips.

"Pretty good, sir. 'Course I'd like to be playin' regular. It's hard going in only now an' then."

"I know, I realize that. I want to find the right spot before I do throw you in, though. This club isn't settled yet, not by no means. Joe, I been learning things about you today. A newspaperman was telling me you ran the one hundred in 9.8 and jumped six feet in high school? That correct?"

"Yes, sir."

"H'm . . . no wonder you're fast. No wonder you grab those liners out there." Grouchy twisted the cigar around in his mouth while he waited, listening. It was plain the old chap hardly knew how to attack the problem before him or where to begin. He cleared his throat and started again. "Joe, you make me think of a kid I played with one season . . . years ago now. Time sure flies, doesn't it? It was back in Davenport in the Three-Eye League, and you remind me of him, same build, same way of handling himself on the field, 'cepting only he was a pitcher. A crazy kid, that boy, wild but one grand ballplayer. He had about everything, fast ball, hook, sinker. Why, he could be up there in the big time winning his fifteen games a year right now if he wasn't so careless. He never took care, never bothered much. Everyone liked him and he horsed around until he horsed himself out of the big leagues. Truth is, this fella's on his way out of baseball now, I think. Maybe you heard of him, fella by the name of Raz Nugent."

The youngster never budged. His lips were tight as they had been when he faced his father that afternoon in the box. His face was hard; he sat quietly. Only the chair betrayed him. It creaked ever so slightly. He said nothing.

Grouchy waited, hoping the boy would open up. When nothing happened he remarked casually, "That was pretty grim out there today, Joe."

"He had it coming." His mouth opened; his mouth shut. Just four words, no more.

Grouchy removed the cigar from his lips, looked at it, stuck it back once more. "Joe, I was never so hot in the big leagues, only played a couple of seasons in the majors; but I know what your pa is going through right now and, believe me, it ain't funny. Especially when you've been a big shot and a star like he was. Why sure, every ballplayer that goes up has to go down. Only it's hard when it comes. You'll find that out some day . . ."

"I'll take it . . . when it comes."

Grouchy felt he would, too, take it better than his father. The boy's face was expressionless save around the eyes. There was dislike, even hatred, in those eyes. The old man leaned toward him.

"Look, son, your father's been a fine ballplayer, a great player, one of the great players of this period, you might say. This afternoon you treated him like a heel." He sat up straight. There it was.

"He *is* a heel."

"Well . . . now . . . maybe . . . only Joe, you don't hit a man when he's down, do you? Your old man's on the way out, you know that. And what's more, you helped things along out there this afternoon."

"I hope so. I know what he put my ma through for twenty years." His hostility increased.

"Yeah, sure, I know. Well, maybe you'll understand things better when you've been through it yourself. Only I'm kinda fond of your pa, Joe, him and me starting out together in Davenport and all that. What you did out there today . . ."

"You want I should strike out 'cause he's my pa?"

"No, no, of course not. I don't mean it that way. I mean the brush-off you gave him coming in from third. Why, the whole field was watching. Nobody likes to see a thing of that kind, son. You didn't need to act that way . . ."

"He had it coming to him."

Grouchy tried another tack. "I know, Joe, I understand. Think I do, anyway. You had some mighty hard times as a boy and your old man didn't help much."

"Didn't help none." He was blazing now. "Left my mother when I was just a kid. Supposed to send us money; huh, fat lot we ever got out of him. Oh, once in a while we'd get a money order for a few bucks; once in a while he'd come through town and coach me, tell me what was wrong with my batting stance or help me with my swing. I'd think he was all right. Then he'd leave town and we wouldn't hear a word for six months or a year.

"There were times when he was kind of a hero to me. I remember once he come home for Christmas, that was the year after he went into the majors, the year he won sixteen games for the Reds. Boy, was I proud of him. My old man, a real big-leaguer. Greatest guy in the world he was to me, with all the kids in town following us to the park where he'd hit fungos and show us how to make a hook slide. He promised me a Louisville slugger and a major-league glove, and then one morning off he went. After he left town I'd go down every day to the post office. For two weeks I pestered the postmistress waiting for that bat and glove. I thought it was a promise. Shucks, I thought older folks always kept their promises to kids. I'll never forget the end of that two weeks when I finally realized it wasn't coming, that he'd forgotten all about it as soon as he got out of town."

Now it was the older man who was uncomfortable. He recalled a few promises of his own, casual remarks made to youngsters that he'd forgotten or neglected. "Oh, that's really tough. Older folks make promises to kids and don't keep 'em . . ."

The boy continued, poured it out bitterly. "Like that it was. Sometimes I'd think he was a hero and mostly I'd just, well, hate the guy. You can't understand." His suffering was apparent on his face, a young face but a face that showed marks upon it.

"H'm, yes, I getcha. I know lots of youngsters who have fathers they don't like, one reason or another. You dislike him and you feel you've gotta show him up; that's natural. But remember one thing. Raz Nugent was raised on a North Carolina farm. I don't honestly guess he ever even had shoes on until he started to play baseball. He got kicked and cuffed around a lot, and a fella gets kinda toughened after experiences of that sort. And after all,

Joe, he's your father. You know he didn't mean you no harm."

"No harm, hey! Only just harm enough to kill my mother, that's all. She cooked in the Railroad Y to keep us alive for three-four years; then she set up that boardinghouse on Summer Street. She slaved to keep that goin' until the day she died, and the doc said she'd worked herself to death. An' all the time he was pulling down big fat salaries. Oh, my mother hated the guy and she had good reason. I hate him, too."

"Yeah, yeah, sure, I understand, that's pretty tough. Old Raz, he didn't do right by you and your mother. But look, Joe, he's your father, and what's more he's on the way out, likely to be out any minute now. You know old Raz is really his own worst enemy. Don't you think, son, don't you believe . . . wouldn't you like to shake hands with him tomorrow, just forget everything . . ."

"No *sir*. I ain't forgetting nothing."

A tough boy. A hard kid, thought Grouchy, although you can hardly blame him. Young, hard, cruel, but it's understandable enough. If he feels that way, there's not much anyone can do about it. "All right, son, you're the doctor. After all, he's your pa. Only he won't be up here too long, boy, and you know what I think? I think some day you'll

be just a mite sorry. Fact is . . . well . . . fact is,
I heard your pa was due for an unconditional release tonight."

"Yessir, an A.P. man, he told me at dinner tonight."

"You knew then! You knew all the time! Well,
he'll be feeling mighty sorry for himself tomorrow.
He'll be mighty darn low tomorrow. Now don't you
want to run up and see him in his room and just let
him know . . ."

"No sir. I hate the guy. I hadn't laid eyes on him
for years until today and I don't care if I never do
again."

There was a sharp knock at the door. "Now
what?" said the manager with a trace of exasperation in his voice. He felt he had failed, that he had
never talked to such a stubborn youngster as Joe
Nugent. "Yeah? Who is it?"

"U.P.," said a brisk voice. The door opened without invitation and a man stepped in. "Mr. Devine,
sorry to bother you. I wanted to check on this story
that young Kennedy is going up to the Yanks on
option. Anything in it?"

"No dice, Jerry. I'll have something for you on
that tomorrow. Call me tomorrow noon."

The man at the door nodded. Then he noticed
young Joe on the chair. "Say, you're Raz Nugent's

son, aren't you? How's it feel, hitting a homer off your old man?"

Joe uncoiled himself from the chair. Same old line. He nodded curtly. "Yeah." He turned toward his boss. "If you don't want anything more, Mr. Devine, I'll be pushing along."

CHAPTER NINE

THINGS changed for Joe as soon as he got into the line-up regularly. He began to like the club, to like Kansas City, and as he liked it he began to play better baseball. His hitting, especially, picked up. He was not long in discovering that he didn't know as much about playing second base as he had once imagined and that Grouchy Devine, laconic by nature, could talk when he had something to say.

One evening, just before the game, the manager summoned him. He was sitting on a wooden chair in his room alone as Joe entered. He looked at the tall youngster standing there before him, respectful yet confident. What he saw, he liked.

"Well, son, how you getting on?"

"All right, Mr. Devine. I got no complaints to make."

"You like old Mac, don't you, boy?"

"Yes sir, him and me gets on first-rate. He throws a true ball, very light. His side-arm flip out of the hole is just a mite heavy, but no real problem to me. I'm learning a lot every day about the way to play second base. He's my idea of the greatest shortstop in the business."

"Well, you'll like him better the more you get used to him. Fact is, Mac is about the best in the league. There isn't a player in the American Association can teach a boy what Mac Sweeny can. Believe me, son, he's taught a-plenty of 'em. Seems like the moment Mac breaks in a new second baseman, someone offers me so much dough I just can't afford to keep him. Son, I want for you to pay close attention, understand? I want you to do what he says. Have you noticed how Mac always seems to be ready and waiting for the ball whenever it's hit? Know why?"

"No sir, not exactly. He anticipates pretty good; he seems to make the hard ones look easy every time."

"Just so. He anticipates. That's because he knows every batter in this league and what his weakness is, where he hits, and also the kind of pitch he's being served. He watches the catcher and follows the signals so he can break the second the ball is thrown. You must learn to do the same thing. Get so you read those signals and know what to expect. Move according to the count and the situation. I haven't any complaint on your batting so far, but you sure have an awful lot to learn about playing second base."

"Yes sir, I realize that, Mr. Devine."

"Well, boy, I think we understand each other then. You're going to be my regular second baseman from now on. That's, of course, if you make good. You know, like everyone on this team knows, it's strictly up to you."

"Of course I appreciate that, Mr. Devine."

"O.K., son. Get out there and get your raps now."

Joe turned and went into the lockers where the players were dressing, coming and going, leaving for the field.

"Hey, kid," someone called across the room to him. "I hear your old man has been picked up by the Brooklyn Dodgers again."

"Old Whale Belly!" There was contempt in his answer as he reached into the shelf of his locker for his glove. "He won't last."

Another teammate remarked, "Nowadays when that team wins one game, it's a winning streak for them."

"Hey, Joe, didja hear what the Giant manager

said when he learned yer pa was coming back to the Dodgers?"

"Nope, whazzat?" The boy turned at the door.

"He says, 'Last night I went to bed a pennant winner. This morning I wake up and find I'm in second place. Spike Russell called Raz Nugent back.' "

All this time over in the American League the Yankees seemed to be getting nowhere fast. Through the early spring and the first part of the summer they had floundered in the lower half of the first division, winning a few games and losing a few, but making little headway toward the pennant. Injuries hurt them, shake-ups did no good, several exchanges with other clubs helped not at all. By midsummer the president of the club taxed Spencer Newman, his manager, with their lack of success, for the fans were growling. The manager turned on him.

"What do you want us to do, bring up Kansas City?"

The president instantly spoke up. "Say, maybe that wouldn't be such a bad idea at that! They're out in front, doesn't look as if any team could catch 'em. No kidding, Spencer, why don't you call up

Grouchy on the phone and see what he can do for you. How 'bout this young Nugent?"

"I have Kent. He's my second baseman."

"Yeah, but you got no one behind him. Anyway, tell me a club that can't use a good utility infielder."

So Spencer Newman, the New York manager, turned to Grouchy Devine. "Grouchy, what can you do for us? Attendance is falling off and the boss is sore. I'd like to get a good relief man and a first-class utility infielder and a couple of pitchers . . ."

"Pitchers? Nosir! I need every one, Spencer. Fact is, I'd like to pick up a couple of extra ones myself if I had some loose cash. I really need every man on this club. But we ought to build up our pitching staff, and if I got the right price I'd be willing to consider letting you take young Nugent up on option."

"You mean Joe Nugent, Raz's boy?" said Newman, playing dumb.

"Yes, I do."

"No thanks. If he's like the old man."

"He isn't. Had a reputation for being wild in Savannah when he came up to me, but I've kept a tight rein on him and he's behaved all right. He's good-natured, even-tempered, and quiet, too. Never showboats, and he's in there trying every minute. Spence, if you want to know what a man is like, talk to his teammates. The boys all swear by him. He never griped when he was in a batting slump at first, and one day after he'd struck out twice he stayed for half an hour after the game, banging balls against the fences. Doesn't complain, is always willing to play anywhere, and gives his best all the time. His manager in Savannah told me he never lost a day down there through sickness, and if he does get ill or injured, by gosh, you don't hear about it."

"H'm . . . pretty young for the big time, isn't he, Grouchy?"

"I'm high on him," said Grouchy laconically. "What's the pennant worth to you and the boss?"

As a consequence of that telephone call, Joe Nugent took a plane the next day for New York. No such thing as a father playing against his son had ever happened in the major leagues, any more than it had in the American Association, but by the end of August it appeared to be at least a possibility. For although he was a youngster among veterans, Joe made good immediately with the Yankees. If he worried out there on the diamond he never showed it, playing with the same nonchalance and competence as he had back in Savannah a few short months before. He was soon carrying his share of the team load and more, saving games by hits in the pinches when they counted most, turning line drives into put-outs and double plays by his speed of foot. His quiet confidence was amazing. Even at his age he had his father's assurance but without the older man's conceit.

Old Stubblebeard related to Casey, the sports columnist, a story of the youngster's poise in a critical game against the Red Sox. Stubblebeard was the plate umpire that day, and the boy was hitting the cripples, but on the 3-1 count he was ordered to take. The pitch was over one corner and the umpire called it a strike, though Joe felt sure it was a ball.

"You won't believe me, Casey, the kid didn't squawk none. He just reproved me, polite-like. 'Sir,' he says, 'I think you missed that pitch.' "

Casey laughed. "What you answer, Stubble?"

"I says, 'Maybe so, son, maybe so. We'll take an extra close look at the next one.' Then he turns and says, 'Yessir, I'd appreciate your doing that.' "

Casey described the upsurge of the Yanks in his column in the *Mail* the next day.

"Ask Spencer Newman what makes the Yankees tick these days and he will say, 'That kid, Joe Nugent, at second base. I honestly don't know where we would be without Nugent. He's been making impossible plays round the bag and bust-ing out in a home-run rash in every ball park in the league. Whatever success we have had, Nugent deserves a major share of the credit. His batting is amazing. Every time I look up from the dugout he's on base. They tell me that since the first week of the month he has hit safely in thirty out of thirty-six games. Nugent lays his success to Grouchy Devine. "Grouchy got me to change my stance a little and told me to try to pull the ball a little more. These two suggestions did the trick. I started to meet the ball and have been very lucky ever since." Well, that's how he puts it. Anyway, he's hitting .360, a pretty substantial gait, and he's carried us right along. Frankly, I don't know how we would have got on without him. He was a gift from heaven.'

"A gift from heaven is perhaps a little strong. Actually he was no gift, because President Billy Rogers of the Yanks paid Grouchy Devine $30,000 for the youngster. However, $30,000 spent as pennant insurance is no fortune. Surely it's the best money the Yanks ever invested. Their hold on first place today is proof of it."

CHAPTER TEN

ONE afternoon that August Raz stalked majestically into the dressing room of the third-place Dodgers in Cincinnati, to be greeted with laughter, shouts, and cries of "Raz!" "Hey there, Razzle," "Oh, Showboat, how are ya?" There were, to be sure, a few half-concealed jeers in the greetings, but as he saluted his former teammates the big chap chose to ignore them. In fact, Raz acted as though the club was in last place and he was doing them a favor by joining.

"Well, gang, here I am. Here's old Raz come back to help you guys out."

"Gonna pitch us into a pennant, Raz? Attaboy!"

"That's correct," answered Razzle with confidence. "I sure am. Don't worry no more."

Same old Razzle, same old Raz, said their glances

across the room to each other. Only occasionally someone looked significantly at Raz's stomach. But even if they weren't exactly counting on him to pitch them into a pennant, they were glad to have him back with them again. Everyone on the club realized that with the old Showboat in their midst, the dressing rooms, hotels, and trains would be cheerier and more amusing places during the tight weeks of the final stretch ahead. It seemed natural to have him sitting in front of his locker before a game, yanking on the two pairs of socks he always wore. Raz was vain, and his thin legs were invariably built up with two pairs of thick stockings.

Bob Russell, the peppy little second baseman, walked over and stuck out his hand. "Mighty glad to see you again, Raz old-timer. We sure missed you."

"Hiya, Bobby, hiya, kid. Thanks lots. I'm happy to see *you*. Say, I gotta son who's gonna make you hustle one of these days. If he keeps on, he'll be the best second baseman in the majors."

"Yeah, I hear he's doing all right for hisself out there in K. C."

"All right!" Raz was shocked. He reached into the pocket of his coat hanging up in the locker and pulled out a wad of newspaper clippings. "All right! I'll say. Looka this." He read from a cutting in his hand. " 'Against the Indianapolis Indians, young Joe scored the winning run again with his timely two-bagger in the ninth. In the second game he was in on three double plays and made sparkling stops all over the infield. Against Columbus the next day he got four for four.' Hear that, son? The feller in the Columbus paper says, 'The best footwork around second base these old eyes have seen for many a long day!' "

"That's fine, Raz, that's grand. You kinda proud of that son of yours, ain't ya?"

"Yes sir, I sure am. He's gonna be one great little ballplayer. In fact, he is right now."

"Does he like his beer as much as you do, Razzle?"

Razzle drew himself up. "He's a mighty good kid. Lemme read what the sports editor of the *Kansas City Star* said last week. Where is that . . . oh, here 'tis. 'Joe Nugent is what is called in baseball parlance a loner. That is, a chap known in the trade as being different from the general run of ballplayers because he seldom pals round with others, reads books not comics, and often goes to the movies alone. Unlike his convivial father who was formerly with Toledo . . .' "

Someone interrupted. "What's that mean, 'convivial,' Razzle?"

"Means I'm a good guy," said Razzle without raising his eyes from the clipping. " 'Unlike his convivial father, he doesn't pal around much with the other players, but everyone respects his industry and willingness to learn.' "

"Hey, Raz," called someone else, "is that correct, that story where he called you Old Whale Belly? Is that straight?"

Raz leaned over his locker, reaching for his shirt. His head was buried in clothes and if he heard the remark he gave no evidence of it. Instead he called to the locker man, "Hey, Chiselbeak! How 'ja expect me to wear a shirt like this? It's about three sizes too small."

The big fellow spent the first part of that hot afternoon on the bench, and during the second part of the double-header went into the bull pen. The score was tied in the ninth when Spike Russell put in a pinch hitter for his starting pitcher and signaled Raz to warm up by holding his arms out in a circle, hands joined before him. The bull pen understood this eloquent gesture, and Raz immediately went to work. When the Reds came in a few minutes later, he strode across the diamond, took the ball from his boss with his customary assurance, and nodded confidently as the manager asked, "Raz, you quite sure you warmed up O.K.? You don't seem warmed up to me."

"Oh yes, yes I am, yes sir, Spike."

He stepped to the mound and threw in his preliminary pitches to Jocko Klein. The batter faced him. After two balls the hitter bunted, and Razzle, once known as the surest fielding pitcher in the league, went over for it, stumbled, half-tripped over his own feet, and misjudged the ball completely.

"Yeah! Have a beer, Raz, have another, old-timer," shouted the bench jockeys with delight.

The next hitter singled sharply to right. The third man to bat promptly put an end to the agony by lifting Razzle's first pitch over the short right-field fence for a homer. The game was finished.

Notwithstanding this shellacking, that evening Raz was his usual confident self in the club car going to New York, kidding and joking with the gang as though he had just pitched a shutout. Stanley Clark of the *Mail*, who was traveling with the club, discovered him there.

"Hey there, Razzle," he called out, "hullo, old-timer. Glad to have you back again. How many no-hitters you aim to throw for us this year?"

Raz took a quick pull on the glass before him. "Two," he replied instantly.

"Two?" The sportswriter stopped, looking at him

attentively. Razzle's face was deadly serious. Say, maybe there's an angle here, thought the newspaperman. "Two! How you figure that out, Raz?"

"That's correct," said Razzle. "One for you, Stan, and one for me."

The gang laughed. Only Spike Russell, sitting near by, observed that the big fellow was drinking Coca-Cola, not beer.

The sportswriter's reaction, shared by the crowd, indicated that Razzle was finished. Spike Russell, watching, said nothing. Directly on arrival in Brooklyn the next morning, Raz started in. When you cannot locate the plate there's only one remedy —work, more work, still more work. In the hottest spell of the summer he reached Ebbets Field early every morning, the first one to show up. When the boys finally arrived, Razzle, who always had to be forced to throw in batting practice, took the mound the minute the nets went up, actually stepping in without being asked. He started refusing beer at night. For dinner he ate one lamb chop, a vegetable, and black coffee. When he found the pounds were not coming off fast enough to suit him, he devised a trick which so amused the gang they came out to the field early on purpose to watch. Raz fastened a rope around his copious stomach and tied the other end to the groundkeeper's tractor.

The driver started up and off they went for a couple of laps around the park, Razzle panting at the end of the rope.

Old Whale Belly! he thought. Old Whale Belly, hey! I'll show that kid up if it's the last thing I do.

Days later, chiefly for lack of any other pitcher, Spike Russell called on Raz to put out the fire in the last innings of a tight game with the Giants. Already the big fellow's control was better, his legs were getting into shape, he was sharper on the mound. In the four innings he pitched he gave only three scattered hits. The crowd yelled after the first inning when, following a single, he set the side down in order and then stalked majestically across the diamond, chucking his glove over the foul line and then leaning down to point it exactly toward third base. This was an old superstition of Razzle's, well known to all Brooklyn fans, and they yelled with delight as the old Showboat went into the dugout. When he finally was retired for a pinch hitter, the crowd rose, applauding his hurling.

All this took time and agony. August came to an end, and slowly the flesh began to come off his huge frame. He dropped from 215 to 205, and finally down to an even 200. As the club left the following week for its last western trip of the season, Razzle was leaner, tougher, trained down to 195, in the best condition he had been in for years.

The Dodgers were not in first place but they were overhauling the leaders. The change in Razzle was evident when he stepped into a game against the Cubs and pitched hitless ball to fourteen men in succession. The next week under a torrid sun in St. Louis, Spike called on him in the tenth in a critical contest. Raz saved the game by striking out two Card sluggers with the bases full. Right then the manager decided to make him a starting pitcher.

The Reds were delighted when he took the mound in Cincinnati the next week, and the bench jockeys went to work on him. Raz enjoyed their jeering. It took exactly three innings and about twenty pitched balls to silence them. As the game progressed and he continued to mow the hitters down, even the rival fans applauded.

When the Dodgers reached home three games out of first place, Raz began to be counted on as a stopper, a guy to throw in to pick up the key games. He needed plenty of rest, but given five or six days between assignments he always came through with a well-hurled job. By the tenth of September with the Brooks crowding the Giants, who were in first place, Raz had five straight wins to his credit.

Meanwhile he kept training carefully, never allowing his exercises and running to fall off. On the trains and in the clubhouse he helped the gang stay loose and amused with his comment and chatter. It was Raz who put red pepper on the coat button of the rookie who always stuck his chewing gum on that button when he went to bat. It was Raz who cheerfully gave interviews beginning, "I love Brooklyn. The fans here are my friends, both of them." And usually ending by predicting a pennant for the Dodgers.

It began to look very possible. Then shortly after their return for the last home stand in the final week of the season, Razzle lost a tough game when the Pirates drove him from the mound in the first of the ninth. Three days later he happened to sit in with the boys in a quiet poker game in Paul Roth's room one hot night. The air was heavy, the boys were ordering and drinking beer, and Raz, who had been on the wagon for weeks, wanted just one beer badly. Then another, and another. The next morning he consumed a breakfast of orange juice.

His head hurt all day. Of course it had to be a time when nothing went right for the Brooks in a critical night game with the Cards. One pitcher was knocked out, a second went in, and then Raz got the finger from Spike. He walked out on the greenness, into that queer make-believe world, to put out the fire. A walk, two doubles, and a single followed in rapid succession until finally the manager came over.

"Raz, you don't look good to me. Gimme that ball." Everyone stood around silently, heads down, saying nothing. There was no chatter and talk around the infield as the new pitcher stepped to the mound. Raz went slowly toward the dugout. The crowd was on him, booing as he went off the field.

"Have another, Raz, have another," yelled the jockeys from the Cardinal bench in great delight.

Within the clubhouse there was a welcome quiet and coolness. The electric fans whirred, air moved, and from inside the rubbing room came the faint noise of a chattering voice from the Doc's portable radio. Raz threw off his clothes in disgust, not concealing his contempt for the fans.

"That's it. You win five straight, help the boys toward a pennant, then you go bad twice in a week and the fans boo you."

"Aw, let 'em holler, Raz; let 'em holler so long as they pay their way into the park," remarked Chisel-beak, the locker man, sweeping up Raz's damp suit in his arms.

"Shoot, the crows got me. I had good stuff to-night; and the time before, too, my arm felt really loose. I was putting the ball where I wanted to put it. A couple of swell pitches against Cushman, and then bang! The next one is up against the fence."

"Yeah, I had good stuff, too." Bonesy Hathaway sat on his bench, a towel around his middle. "Yep, I had good stuff and good control, and the Cards got to me in an inning and a half. Well, that's how baseball is."

"Hey Raz," a voice called from the showers. "You see what your kid said about that interview with Casey, the one where you said we'd win the pennant and pin the Yankees' ears back in the Series?"

"Naw," said Raz. "Untie my shoes, will ya, Chisel? Seems like I can't stoop over today."

"He laughed and called you the 'All-American Adenoid.' Said you wouldn't last."

Apparently Raz didn't hear. He was leaning over with Chisel, wrestling himself out of his shoes.

CHAPTER ELEVEN

THE pennant, they tell you, is not decided on one day of the season, but in all one hundred and fifty-four of them. Yet there were the Dodgers and the Giants all tied up on the last afternoon of the season, with the National League title still undecided. The Yanks, who had won their flag ten days previously, were taking things easy, watching their rivals beat each other's brains out.

That last game, which was to decide whether the old pro and the rookie star would face each other in the Series, was on a Sunday. Most of the regulars on the Yankees were excused that afternoon and decided to visit the Polo Grounds to get a look at their opponents. It took considerable effort to get in, because all New York, New Jersey, and Connecticut had the same idea, but seven of the Yankees managed to obtain seats. One of them was Joe Nugent.

The night before that last game Razzle had saluted his boss as he was leaving the clubhouse for the day with the coaches.

"Hey there, big boy, hey there, Spike! I'll be ready tomorrow if you need me." Some players might have felt diffident about suggesting themselves as the starting pitcher in a critical contest; not Raz Nugent. The old Showboat had never forgotten that remark of the Giant manager when Spike had brought Raz back in August. Nothing would please him more than to take the mound and keep the mound and keep the Giants from a pennant.

"You O.K., are you, Raz?" said Spike, glancing at him reflectively, seeing the change in his appearance since he had returned to the club, a change that he never would have imagined possible. It's a funny game, he thought. You think you know something about ballplayers, and then a man comes back and gets to be a first-string pitcher again after he's supposed to be through. It's sure a funny game.

"Yessir. I'll be there if you want me, Spike. You know I never did mind the Polo Grounds when my fast one was hopping. Old Raz can make those long-ball hitters smack it straight there, and so long as we got Highpockets and that-there kid from Tomkinsville in the gardens, we don't need to worry none. Ya see, the batters can't get their clubs around quick enough to paste the ball into the seats."

Spike stood there, thinking, wishing the responsibility for choosing the starting pitcher for the next game was not his. It was a tough choice, because most of his hurlers were stiff, sore, and lame. Raz sounded fine, of course, but after those last starts . . . So he merely nodded and went out. The next day he finally settled on Homer Slawson, a reliable stand-by, and sent Raz to the bull pen with three other pitchers.

Up in the stands at the Polo Grounds Joe and the other Yankee players watched with interest.

"Looks like yer old man'll get a relief job, if he shows at all, Joe."

"Yeah," answered young Joe, his gaze fixed on the big man in the Dodger uniform, throwing to a catcher. It was his father all right, old Showboat. Yet it was not old Showboat at all. This man wasn't the fat, flabby old pitcher off whom he had hit a homer in Kansas City back in July. Joe had heard stories of his loss of weight, but he had discounted them. He had heard that Raz always dropped from ten to twelve pounds on a hot afternoon and soon put them on again. But this man was different. There was a difference in his face, in his quick walk, and in the loose, easy way he burned in his warm-up pitches. Joe said nothing; he thought plenty. Could his mother have been entirely right, he wondered? Was his father the wastrel, the careless, characterless playboy she had always made him out to be? For the first time he began to see his father in a different light, for Joe was enough of a ball-player to realize how much more difficult it is for an old-timer to come back than for a youngster to come up.

Then the game began. Raz walked out to the bull pen, while tall, lanky Homer Slawson stepped to the mound, facing a packed stadium. Both teams were on their toes, so the pitchers had no trouble keeping hits scattered, although the Giants were getting more wood to the ball and threatening much of the time. They earned one run in the sixth, the Dodgers evened things with a lucky run in the seventh when the New York center fielder misjudged a fly that went for two bases, and Spike Russell brought him home with a droopy single to right. Things were unchanged through the eighth and up until the last of the ninth.

Then the first Giant batter took hold of one of Homer's slants and smacked it to deep right center for a triple. Spike immediately turned and signaled the bull pen, while the crowd rose, anxiously watching to see who was coming in. The four Dodger pitchers paid no attention to the call, still throwing furiously, until finally Steamboat Jackson, the first-base umpire, walked angrily toward them, calling and beckoning.

"Old Showboat? Nope . . . yes . . . by gosh, he's giving yer pa the finger, Joe," said one of the Yankees with interest. "Well, if Razzle shuts them out now, believe me, he's good. I'll hand it to him." They all glanced down the row at the young Nugent who was watching, lips together. He was silent; he knew well what it meant to enter an important game at such a minute.

Raz came across the grass. No slouching, no shuffling to the mound; his step was brisk and confident. As he neared the diamond, greeted by that great roar from the crowd, only by the occasional tug at the peak of his cap could you see that he felt the strain. The appeals of the Brooklyn fans, the taunts and jeers from the Giant bench, the clap-clapping of the New York rooters, the dangerous situation with that white figure perched on third base—all this was meat and drink to him. This was the big moment. Razzle knew it. He made the most of it.

"Nugent, number 14, now pitching for Brooklyn."

There was a note of appeal in Spike Russell's

voice as he handed Raz the ball. "Get us out of this jam, Razzle. Get us out of it, boy."

"O.K., Spike," grunted Raz, throwing the ball he had taken from his manager to the plate. He spoke over his shoulder between his warm-up pitches. "Skipper, if old Raz ain't worrying none, you shouldn't be neither."

On Spike's orders, Jocko Klein stepped aside to pass the leading hitter of the Giants. Then Raz went to work.

All this time Joe was quiet, but he was watching and thinking. Why, the old man has it still; he still has his curve and his fast ball! He still has it. Even from the stands it was plain that he was loose and relaxed, that his curve was snapping. Joe's eyes narrowed as Raz clipped the outside corner for a strike, then threw another strike as the Giant fans yelled, appealing to the batter for a long ball, any ball out of the infield.

But it was evident that Raz, who had once been a rear-back-and-blaze-'em-through pitcher, had become foxier with age. Now he had control. Throwing in a change-of-pace, he caught the batter off balance and struck him out.

Joe shook his head. "Say," he remarked half to himself, "say, he's no pushover. No sir, he isn't." He leaned forward, elbows on knees, watching in-

tently as his father took the ball from Spike Russell
and went to work with one man gone. Joe could see
that his down-breaking stuff was sneaky fast, evidently aimed to keep the ball on the ground and
prevent the man on third from scoring after a deep
fly to the far reaches of the Polo Grounds outfield.
But the hitter had orders to squeeze the runner in,
and tried a bunt. Skillfully he pushed a perfect slow
roller toward first base.

Raz was on the ball like a hawk, his anticipation
perfect, his footwork beautiful. He saw instantly it
was too late to try for the man at the plate. So he
went for their only chance, the double play, the one
that has lost more games than any in baseball—
pitcher-to-second-to-first. He gunned the ball in fast
and accurately to Spike Russell at second.

Then he did an amazing thing.

Instead of waiting, instead of watching to see the
finish of the play, he turned and walked toward the
bench, tossing his glove in front of him. Joe's eyes
followed the old Showboat as he reached the foul
line, leaned over, and carefully pointed the glove
toward third. In the roar that followed from the
stands, it was hard to tell whether the crowd was
yelling approval of that split-second double play
that pulled the Dodgers back into the game and the

pennant race, or Razzle's gesture of bravado as he walked to the dugout.

One of the Yankees in the stands slapped his knee. The words were spoken in a grudging tone but they were sincere. "Hang it, the old guy's really got it. Hey there, Joe, hey there! I never knew he had that much stuff before! Joe . . ." He called down the row to the boy, who was concentrating on the scene in the Brooklyn dugout where the Dodgers were mauling and hauling and slapping his father on the back, hugging him to their sweaty chests. "Hey, Joe, yer old man's one hell of a pitcher still, d'you know that?"

Joe Nugent nodded. He was puzzled and disturbed, as one always is when a fixed opinion of someone is proved wrong. Joe was not the only person in the Polo Grounds whose preconceived ideas of Raz Nugent, the old pitcher, were undergoing considerable revision.

From then on, it was merely a question of when the Dodgers would score. Old Raz had the Giants completely under control. In the tenth, eleventh, twelfth, he gave up one base on balls and one scratch single. Mixing up his pitches, shooting over his change-of-pace and then bearing down with his fast one, he had the New York batters handcuffed so that they were unable to get the ball out of the infield. The one man who got on, with a slow, dragged roller toward second base, was cut down stealing by Jocko's sharp throw. In the twelfth, Raz struck out the last two men with their bats on their shoulders. As he did so, one of the Yankee players in the stands emitted a long, sharp whistle. It spoke volumes, that whistle.

In the Dodgers' half of the thirteenth, High-pockets McDade, the first batter, lined a drive to left center.

"Go for three, Hi, go for three, kid," shouted the coaches, as he roared around the bases and slid safely into third. Spike Russell brought him home with a fly to right which was too deep even to warrant a throw-in, and after the side was retired Raz took the mound again.

This is it, thought Joe, this is the test; if he blows up, he's the same old Razzle.

The throngs of Giant fans howled and yelled, shrieking at him, ringing bells and blowing horns, hoping he would tire or explode or go to pieces. Instead, he did nothing of the sort. He carefully pitched the Dodgers into a pennant by retiring the side in order, putting out the last man himself when he covered first and took the throw from the first baseman on a hard-hit ball to the right.

When Casey, the sportswriter, left the park, he

happened by chance to overtake the little knot of Yankees, seriously discussing the afternoon's events. It was plain that, like other fans, their opinion had been changed by what had happened that day. He wormed his way through the crowd and caught up with them, anxious to get a couple of good quotes for his next day's column. The first man he reached was young Joe.

"Joe! Say, Joe! Hey, Nugent, what you think 'bout Old Whale Belly now?"

To the sportswriter's astonishment, the boy turned on him quickly. "Whad'ya mean, Old Whale Belly? He's down to a hundred and ninety pounds, so they tell me. You saw him out there this afternoon, Casey! Why don't you try hitting against that stuff yourself?"

He passed along quickly. The sportswriter stood jostled by the moving throng, looking after him with amazement. Gosh, he thought, and six weeks ago he was calling his old man the All-American Adenoid!

CHAPTER TWELVE

PEOPLE think a World Series starts when the umpire calls "Play ball." It starts long before that. It starts in midsummer when some reporter writes that the club has a good chance for the pennant. It starts after a crucial game in September when the club beats its chief contender in the tenth inning. It starts in earnest after each team wins the flag, or even before that, when the managers send their scouts out to follow the other club, when the skipper and the coaches begin planning and figuring and setting up their strategy, when the sportswriters and radio men and photographers come around hand-shaking the winners. It begins then and lasts all day every day, and for some players all night, building up, getting bigger and bigger as game time draws near.

For the freshmen, for those rookies who have never played before eighty thousand fans or scooped up a line drive with a six-thousand-dollar tag on it, the enormity of it is frightening. You say to yourself, Shoot, it's just another ball game. Those guys pull on their pants one leg at a time, same's we do. You say these things. But in your heart you know it isn't so.

Now the entire nation was absorbed by the clash between the Nugents, the father and the son who disliked each other. Folks who had never cared for sport, who had not followed baseball for years, watched the newspapers every day and planned to listen to the World Series on the radio.

There were long lines of standees at the gates when Joe reached the park early on the morning of the first game. Inside, the vast reaches of the Yankee Stadium were already filling slowly with those restless, heaving thousands, always in motion, always apparently shifting from place to place. The stands were covered with flags and bunting, making it seem a different ball park. Even the players in their new white and gray uniforms looked strange. Clowns pretended to play baseball. Swing bands blared out in the stands. A freak hung by his ankles and hit fungos. Over everything was the continuous noise, the fever of excitement which told you plainly enough that this was not just an ordinary game but a very special occasion. The World Series!

But it was even more than just that; it was the first time a father and son had ever met in the Series. This was Nugent against Nugent, the father and son who were enemies. That was the angle of the reporters and radio commentators who surrounded both Joe and Raz at practice, the dream of the camera men who chased them on the field. The two were taken in half a dozen different poses, shaking hands, Joe waving a bat menacingly in his father's face, and the favorite of them all—the one in which Razzle stood with an apparently affectionate arm around Joe's shoulder. It was plain this was one pose that the youngster did not enjoy. So much fuss was made over them that it almost seemed as though they were more important than the battle between the two ball clubs.

Then the umpires, six of them, strolled out from the dressing quarters. At last came *The Star-Spangled Banner,* and then the big Yankee pitcher on the rubber burned in his final warm-ups as his teammates took the field. Finally there was a hush, a second's silence over the vast scene. The Series was about to begin.

For three innings the two teams felt each other

out like two boxers in a ring, cautiously and gingerly, the batters hitting balls without eyes on them, balls that went straight at the fielders, the pitchers on both sides breaking their curves well ahead of the men at the plate. Up to the fourth, neither team had scored or even threatened to score, and Joe Nugent had not handled a ball save to toss it around the infield after a put-out. Starting the fourth, Bob Russell worked the Yankee pitcher for a pass, the first Dodger to get on. With the pitcher up, everyone expected a sacrifice of some sort. The Yankee first and third basemen came charging in on each pitch. When the count reached two strikes and a ball, the Dodgers tried the hit-and-run. Elmer McCaffrey at the plate sent a slow, hopping roller between first and second, the easiest kind of a chance. Joe saw the speedy baserunner fly past to second and realized there was no chance for a double play. With the heavy pitcher lumbering toward first there was little hurry or pressure upon him, so he met the ball with complete confidence, just as he had met a thousand others, ready to scoop it up and throw the hitter out. A simple enough chance, a routine play, the kind of a hopper you can't miss.

The kind you invariably do miss. The ball came toward him, and in some inexplicable manner rolled through and out into short right field.

The right fielder rushed in to cover. Joe himself backtracked after the ball at full speed, while from the coaching boxes came the cries of the Dodger coaches. Bob Russell, a speedster on the base paths, rounded second without hesitating and pounded on into third.

It was a race for the ball, a tight race between Joe and his right fielder, and the younger man was first to reach the ball as it rolled and bobbled along, halfway between them. He grabbed at it, picked it up, turned, and threw. The throw was hurried and wild. The third baseman jumped and tipped the ball so that it sailed behind him to the stands. Once again two Yankees chased after it, while Bob Russell went on in to score, and Elmer McCaffrey took second easily.

Tommy Zimmerman, the Dodger first baseman, hit a drive against the fence which brought Elmer in. Roy Tucker then lifted one of the pitcher's slants into the stands, and within three minutes the score was four to nothing, the Yankee hurler was taking an early bath, the despised Dodgers were pounding the stuffing out of their rivals, and the stands were in a ferment.

An hour and ten minutes later, a Pinkerton man was standing beside the Yankee dressing-room door. Casey, as was his habit after an important game, went back to get the players' reaction. He started to enter, but the blue-coated guard reached out and caught him sharply by the arm.

"Where you think you're going, Bud?"

Casey drew himself up, that is, insofar as his short stature would permit. After all, he was the columnist of the *Mail*, a veteran sportswriter, known to practically everyone around the Stadium and other ball parks, too; for it was his boast that he could go up to any press gate in the nation and get through merely by greeting somebody there by his first name.

"Where you think I'm going? I'm gonna interview the players. Think I do this for fun? What's up, Mac? Wanna see my press card?"

"You ain't goin' in there, Bud."

"Whad'ya mean I ain't goin' in?"

"Orders. Newman says no one's allowed in the dressing room at all today."

"I'm not no one. I'm Casey of the *Mail*."

"You're no one to me, mister. I don't care if you're the President, no newspaperman nor anyone else gets in this dressing room tonight."

Casey paused. Sometimes after critical games managers make a rule that five minutes or even ten must elapse before reporters are admitted to the clubhouse, but seldom that he could remember had anyone shut the boys out completely. However, after the debacle of that afternoon he couldn't wonder. Casey lit a cigarette and stood watching. Already two other expostulating reporters were arguing with the Pinkerton man who stood leaning against the door, one arm high on the frame, barring the way.

The scene inside the clubhouse was gloomy indeed. The Yanks were down. Like every badly beaten team, they were tired. No one said much, but their faces expressed their feelings. Joe Nugent sat on his bench, head down, wrapped in misery. Here and there someone kicked a shoe against his metal locker with a resounding bang that reflected their disgust and despair. To be beaten was surely no disgrace. To be shut out 7-0 in a one-sided game was humiliating, especially by the Dodgers, especially when they had been 5 to 1 favorites before the game. Even genial Spencer Newman couldn't force a smile. He shook his head as he wearily pulled off his shoe.

"The boys were putting them into the stands in practice; they must have lost two dozen balls out there before the game. But the hitting was missing when it paid off."

A Yankee coach nodded. "We sure didn't have it today, boss. That McCaffrey was hotter than a two-dollar pistol. He had just about everything. I'll swear he got faster the longer he pitched."

Newman pulled off his other shoe. "Let's forget it. Don't say anything to the kid, Hank. Take him out to dinner and try and cheer him up. He feels bad enough as it is. Tomorrow's another day."

No reporters were shut out of the Dodger dressing room where a different scene was taking place. Here was laughter, and the shouts of the conquerors were audible even in the big concrete hallways. Inside everything was in disorder. Towels were thrown around the room; players were scrambling back and forth, thumping each other with enthusiasm. The air was thick with smoke from the photographers' flash bulbs. Everyone was talking and the place was noisy with talk and yelling.

"Hit a change-up pace for that one. It was a little outside but I got some wood on it." "Shucks, is those the great Yankees! They didn't show nothing." "We oughta take four straight." "Wonder if they'll put in Fuller tomorrow. If they do, boy, we'll smear him like we smeared those guys today."

"Dunno. I shan't make up my mind who I'll pitch until game time tomorrow. What's that? Yep, Mc-Caffrey had it today. Well, you all know baseball. They may turn round and bat our brains out next time. Yes, I'll stand on this line-up; it seemed to work today. No, I won't say anything about him. And look, fellers, please don't ask Raz about his boy. He feels terrible about it; he feels almost like he made those errors himself."

Hank Kleinholz, an old Yankee coach, took young Joe to dinner alone. They went to a quiet restaurant in a side street where they sat in silence, both men thinking of the ruined afternoon. Hank tried to make conversation, but the boy was far too miserable to respond and even the dinner which he ate helped very little. He reached his room in the hotel about eight-thirty. Four or five players were sitting around, among them Burwell Kent, who until Joe's arrival from Kansas City had been the regular Yankee second baseman. It was evident that some of the boys had been loosening up. Moreover, even after that afternoon's disaster their attitude toward the Dodgers still bordered on contempt.

"Call themselves a ball club," said one voice with scorn.

Joe Nugent hung up his coat and went over to one of the beds, now littered with newspapers. The one thing in the world he didn't want to see was a newspaper, but there it was in front of him. There was Bob Russell rounding second base and his own figure half-turned, starting to run after the ball trickling along the grass behind him.

"Nuts," said another voice. "What do you expect when their best pitcher is Razzle Nugent? Why, he's the guy who carried them through to a pennant. That right, Joe? What can you expect of a team like that?"

Joe leaned back on the bed.

"Yeah," he said noncommittally.

Burwell Kent spoke up. There was contempt in his voice.

"That pa of yours is a card all right, but he ain't no ballplayer. Years ago when he was with the Pirates I understand the club had to send his check down home to his wife. One day Razzle showed up considerably the worse for wear and when the manager said it was his turn to pitch, Raz said, 'Not me! Get my wife in there to pitch for me. You've given her my dough anyway.'"

The long-legged boy on the bed stiffened. No one in the room, however, noticed it. He spoke quietly. "That ain't true," he said.

"I hear 'tis," continued the other man. "I had it straight from Billy Fox of the Pirates. He oughta . . ."

"I say it ain't true."

Kent should have recognized the menacing lift in his tone. Kent wasn't drunk, but his wits were not functioning as well as usual. Without sensing the boy's irritation, he went along amiably. "What is he? Just a bum anyway. He's been with every club in the circuit and been thrown out of every hotel . . ."

"He's no bum. He's one swell pitcher and you may find it out before this Series is over."

"I say old Raz is a bum. I say he's a big bag of wind. I say if I was in there I'd sure flatten him out. He never was any good and never will be. He's just a bum."

Joe leaped from the bed.

"You take that back!" He edged up close to where Burwell Kent was leaning against an armchair. "You take that back! Raz Nugent is my old man."

"I don't care if he is your old man."

"Sit down, Burwell."

"Aw, leave the kid be!"

"Let him alone, Burwell!"

"You take that back." The boy's voice was hard, quiet, businesslike.

Perhaps Kent resented losing his place to this youngster. Perhaps it was the beers he had enjoyed before dinner. Perhaps it was the fact, although young Joe didn't know it, that he had been a small-time fighter before he took up baseball and was sure of himself in any rough-and-tumble. There was scorn in his voice, his lip curled. "Aw, he's a bum! Always was, always will be."

Suddenly Joe Nugent slapped him across the face, slapped him so hard that the other man went reeling back. He tottered, righting himself against the armchair, sprang forward, and caught Joe full on the mouth. The boy fell back, clutching his jaw. Burwell Kent, a dentist without a license, had knocked out two front teeth with one punch.

CHAPTER THIRTEEN

DURING a World Series, with dozens of news hawks hunting in every corner for an angle and working like fury to uncover a lead, news gets around quickly. The episode that night didn't take long to get out. One man mentioned it to his roomie, who casually dropped a hint to some friend, who ran into a sportswriter in the hotel lobby. And the hunt was on. If a single reporter gets a clue, twenty by some miraculous seventh sense are soon on the trail. Telephones jingle, questions are asked, managers and coaches are routed from bed, and before long, incidents that may have been comparatively harmless are built up and magnified. Though no morning newspaper told the exact story, several writers hinted at a row among prominent members of the Yankees the previous evening, and even spoke of dissension hovering over the club.

It didn't take long for the whole yarn to reach the Brooklyn clubhouse. By this time the brawl had become a general fist fight, with half the Yankee team out on the floor. Only one thing was needed— proof. The proof, it was said, would be visible on Joe Nugent's face that morning.

So naturally everyone looked at him with interest and attention when he appeared on the field at eleven o'clock. There it was, plain for everyone to see, the swollen lip, the gap in the front teeth when- ever he opened his mouth. The Dodgers glanced at each other significantly. It was all the bench jockeys needed.

The Yanks that second afternoon were down but not out. They came back with Jake Stein, a 22-game winner, who had been their stopper all season. Spike Russell felt himself on top with the first con- test in the bag and several good pitchers in reserve, so he determined to gamble with old Razzle. If he lost he was still even, with his best starters ready to go the next day; if he managed to win, he was in an almost unbeatable position.

It was a real battle all the way, both pitchers in fine form, holding the hitters to a few scattered singles. In the first inning came the event the crowd was looking for, and the whole nation was watching—young Nugent against old Nugent. Here it was at last. This, quite as much as the team struggle, was what most of the fans wanted to see. They noted intently every move of the two players. Will the rookie make good? Will the father give him an easy one to hit? Will the big pitcher stand by his teammates and strike him out? Do they really dislike each other, as the sportswriters all say? These were a few of the questions everyone in the park wanted answered.

Suddenly, as Joe stepped to the plate in the tense quiet, came jeers from the Dodger bench, from the Brooklyn players in the field. Never known for their reticence toward opponents, that afternoon they let him have it from every side. With distinct clearness, their voices came to him as he stepped to the plate.

"Hey, Joe, who's yer dentist?"

"Joe, been to the dentist lately?"

"Hey, where's my front teeth? Oh, Ma, where's my front teeth?"

Joe tried hard to appear unconscious of those voices, to pretend he hadn't heard. He was not too successful. Out on the mound the big man peered down, nodding with confidence at his catcher behind the plate, apparently at ease with the world, sure of himself.

Nugent against Nugent. This was it! Raz stepped to the rubber, wound up. It was a fast ball, waist-high, so fast that Joe swung late and behind it. Strike one!

Next the pattern called for a wasted pitch, but Joe knew his father was following no pattern, and set himself. Sure enough, once again it was a fast ball, this time low. For the second time he swung too late and missed. Strike two!

As Joe expected, Razzle wasted the following pitch. He could afford to waste one, and the boy, feeling like an uncertain artisan before an old master, knew it. He also realized that the old Showboat loved this moment—the cheers and yells from the stands, the drama of the Series, perhaps even the chance to rub in his comeback. He took plenty of time, fingering the rosin bag, hitching at his pants, rolling the ball in the palm of his hand, making Joe wait until the last, final second. Playing with him, almost.

Joe at the plate scuffed the dirt nervously, annoyed with his father and with himself for being annoyed. He watched carefully as the long left leg came up, pivoted, and the white sphere zoomed toward him. The crowd started to shriek as it began its journey. Joe stood paralyzed while the ball snapped across the outer corner. Strike three! He was caught window-shopping and cut down.

A volume of noise rang out over the stands, cheers came from the Brooklyn rooters. Joe returned to the Yankee bench, slinging his bat ahead of him in disgust.

"What's he got, Joe?" called one of the batters about to step out of the dugout. There was a trace of anxiety in his tone which the boy noticed.

"He's got control that he didn't have three months ago, that's what he's got. And he's fast, sneaky fast, for another thing," replied the boy, slumping to a seat. "He's faster'n most of the guys in our league, faster to me than Kissell of the A's or Crane of the Sox, anyhow. He chucks one here and one there, and you can't figure what's coming next. Shucks, I was late swinging on those first two."

There he sat, watching disconsolately as Raz mowed down the Yankee hitters, both the top and the bottom of the batting order. Slider, sinker, screwball, the old chap had them all. Rested and fresh, he was sharp that afternoon, and he was ahead of the batters most of the way. The Yanks finally got their first run of the Series and their first in fifteen innings with a single, followed by a sacrifice and a line drive to left in the sixth. The Brooks came back with two runs in their half of the seventh, and the score remained 2-1 in the eighth and the ninth.

Then with the crowd on its feet, the two teams reached the last of the ninth. The Dodger bull pen, which had been busy all through the game, went hotly into action, balls flying back and forth from catchers to pitchers, bang-bang, bang-bang. Raz got the first batter on a fly to center. He struggled a long while with Tracy Jones, who kept smacking long fouls down the right-field line. Then he lifted a foul fly deep and out of play to the right. Joe, who was waiting in the circle to bat next, saw Tommy Zimmerman, the Dodger first baseman, charge over, head up, determined to get that ball. He charged desperately, reached out, caught it, and smacked into the low iron rail of the boxes with a sound Joe could plainly hear. Tumbling over, he came up, limping badly, the ball in his mitt.

Old Raz rushed off the mound and came running toward the plucky first baseman as he hobbled toward the diamond. Zimmerman tossed the ball to his pitcher underhand, and Joe saw his father's face close to, noticed that he was tired, drawn, weary. He watched as Razzle put one arm around Zimmerman and clapped him affectionately on the back. Now the Yankees were only a single put-out away from their second straight loss in the Series.

Joe took his place at the plate. Once again the Dodger bench jockeys were on him as he stepped in. No one was leaving yet, the exits were uncrowded, for everyone realized that Joe was a dangerous man, and that a single run could change the whole contest. This time he shut his ears to the bench shouters at his back; he was set and determined. For he had batted three times that afternoon, struck out once and hit two weak grounders. This time he was coming through.

Perhaps the older man was tiring. Perhaps, as Joe hoped, he was a bit overconfident. Possibly he thought he had the youngster in his pocket. At any rate, on the second pitch Joe caught one of his slants cleanly on the wood, and exploded a murderous drive to deep right center between the two fleet Dodger fielders.

Head down, the boy raced around the path. He cut over first at a terrific rate, tore into second going all out, got the green light from the third-base coach who was watching Roy Tucker and Highpockets chase the ball against the fence. It was the latter who got there first, turned and gunned it in to Bob Russell far out on the grass. From Bob the throw was straight and true to the man astride the bag at third. Ball and runner seemed to arrive together in a cloud of dust. But Joe, lying on the ground, knew he was safe and, looking up, saw the third-base umpire with his hands down.

Instantly the man in blue was surrounded. Spike Russell, who had been backing up, roared over. He charged toward the umpire with loud outcries. So did Jocko Klein, who also had been backing the throw, while Charlie Draper, the coach, rushed from the dugout. Now half a dozen players encircled the little man, all sore, angry, sure they were right, certain Joe was out. The third baseman stuck his face up against the umpire's. Someone yanked him back and he wormed his way in once more. Then the umpire folded his arms and walked off a few feet.

All the while, Joe stood on the bag, dusting off his trousers, happy and content at last. The soreness inside had vanished as he circled those bases. Finally he was content. He knew he had it; now the proof was there for everyone in the park to see. Even the awful throbbing of his mouth, which had kept him awake all night and had lasted most of the morning, vanished. He straightened up. From the bench his teammates were holding up clasped hands to congratulate him. Forgotten were his bobbles of the previous day. Now he was with them again. The Yankees were on the way back. Out in the field the Dodger fly catchers stood panting, for it had been one of the longest, cleanest hits of the Series.

The knot around the umpire finally dissolved. From third Joe saw the first baseman rub his battered leg. Now Joe understood as never before the importance of every single play in a ball game. But for that catch, Tracy Jones might have reached first base and the game would now be tied.

Was it the beginning of the end for his father? Out in the bull pen still another hurler threw off his jacket and went to work. Would they take the old man out? As Joe watched, Spike Russell walked across to the box, stood there talking a minute, looking up earnestly into the big fellow's face.

No, he's sticking with him! He's going to let him finish the game. And here I am, ninety feet from a tie, with the winning run at the plate.

The stands were frenzied now, some yowling for a new pitcher, others yelling just to upset Raz, others from the sheer tenseness of the moment. One of the leading batters on the Yankees stepped in. Joe stood over the bag, watching his father face the new man at the plate, seeing him make that characteristic twitch at the peak of his cap, walk away from the mound, lean over to finger the rosin bag with a trembling hand. He tossed it to one side. At

last he seemed ready to take the mound and receive his signals.

Joe moved two feet off the bag, watching carefully, took another stride, arms out, ready for anything. At least he thought he was ready for anything. Then two things hit him. One was a fearful,
a dreadful shriek from Hank, the third-base coach,
behind him. The other was a stiff, ugly punch in
the ribs that met him just as his reflexes warned
him to jump for the bag and safety. It was a jab at
his side that really hurt. He looked around, annoyed, surprised, astonished by the mighty roar
which swept the whole park.

The hidden ball trick! The oldest gag in baseball
had been pulled on him for the third out. In the
ninth inning of a World Series game!

He stood there foolishly while the triumphant
Dodgers swarmed past. Old Raz was instantly surrounded by half a dozen teammates. Now they were
half-carrying, half-hauling him off the field.

Only one or two noticed Joe as they ran past,
exultation on their faces, calling over their shoulders
at him, "Hey, Joe, hey there, Joe-boy, how's yer
dentist, fella?"

CHAPTER FOURTEEN

ALL night long Joe lay awake feeling that poke in his ribs, still tender where the Dodger third baseman had jabbed him; all night he felt that horrible sensation which came over him as he saw the ball in the man's glove and realized what had happened. Like the whole Yankee team, he had come into the Series overconfident, sure of American League superiority, certain of his own ability even in these big moments of baseball. Then with everyone watching he had flivvered badly. Tagged by press and radio as the Yankee rookie star, as the man who had helped them to the pennant, he had stumbled and bumbled, made errors in the field, and finished the first two games with the mighty batting average of .125. Worst of all, he'd been caught at a vital moment by the oldest gag in the game.

Joe twisted and turned, playing the game over
and over, especially that irretrievable ninth inning,
cursing himself, blaming the coach and then cursing
himself once more, and twisting and turning again.
Dawn finally came to Manhattan. The start of another day.

The Dodgers ought to have been stale and worn
after their bruising battle for the pennant. Yet they
had been keen and on their toes. Whereas the
Yanks, too sure of their superiority, were let down
by the time lag between their victory in the American League and the start of the Series. Or so everyone said. So the sportswriters told you. All this was
plain enough afterward. Yet the odds beforehand
had been 20 to 1 against the Dodgers winning even
the first game.

By now it was apparent that the Yankees had
been badly shaken. One of their star pitchers had
been clawed from the box and they had been
beaten the second time in a well-played contest.
Now they were in the hole. They needed that third
game in Brooklyn. In fact, they had to have it.

Perhaps, speculated some sportswriters, they had
looked on the Dodgers as easy money merely because Razzle was one of their best pitchers. Yet the
old Showboat had proved to the Yanks why he was
a winner, why he had helped the Brooks in the

stretch. And the Yankee hitters, where had they gone? And those fielding stars, that strength in the outfield, that wonderful infield with young Joe Nugent performing miracles around second base. As Casey put it in his column, "So far, anyhow, Joe Nugent can't carry little Bobby Russell's glove. They shouldn't be compared."

The writers who had gone out on a limb for the Yanks before the Series now switched en masse to the Dodgers. Why not, indeed? Spike Russell, they suggested, was in a strong position. He had gambled early in the Series with old Raz, had won, and still had two first-class pitchers to throw against his rivals—Homer Slawson and Bones Hathaway. Homer was that rarity, a southpaw with control, a tough man for a team of left-handed batters like the Yanks. But they had to beat him somehow.

So far the Series had been fairly uneventful save for the two unexpected Dodger victories. The stars had failed to shine. Joe Nugent had become merely another nervous and uncertain freshman. There had been few sensational plays in the field and little real hitting to bring the fans to their feet, yelling.

Spike Russell, standing behind the batting cage before the game, shrugged his shoulders at a question from Casey about the Yankee power. "I'd rather give credit to our pitchers. Elmer and Raz have been very good. That old guy needs rest, but he's a fine pitcher when he's right. He was great, just great, out there yesterday. And he sure knows baseball. Don't spread this round, Casey, but the boss has him slated to manage one of our important farm clubs next year."

"No! That right? Bet I know which one, but I won't guess. Thanks, Spike. Ya know, I've followed baseball for years, and I've never seen a comeback like the old Showboat made this season."

"Well, he had a reason."

"How you mean—the boy?"

"Yes, sir. He was determined to show the kid he still had it."

"Kid isn't doing so good. I wonder why Newman didn't put the screws on after what happened the other night. Although everyone has a different version of that affair. Spike, what's the matter with the boy, d'you think? And with all those Yanks? They don't seem the real Yanks to me. They're kinda uncertain out there, sort of dazed . . ."

"You'd be dazed too, Casey. We rocked them back on their heels with a quick punch and then caught them yesterday with a left to the jaw before they'd righted themselves completely," said Spike, a boxing fan. "But look here, don't underestimate that team, don't kid yourself; they may explode any minute. Believe me, I'm worried. I lay awake last night . . ."

"He's worried! He lay awake last night!" said Spencer Newman, the Yankee manager, half an hour later when Casey quoted Spike's words to him. "Believe me, I'd like to be in that terrible spot he's in, two games up and his two best pitchers fresh and rested. There's no pleasing some folks. We're lucky to be on the field with 'em this afternoon."

Yet notwithstanding his pessimism, explode was just what the Yankees did that day. They erupted all over the place. Homer Slawson proved to be worn down by the season's grind and the tight finish of the National League pennant race, and the Yankees, on the warpath from the start, found him no puzzle. They pushed over a run in the first, and broke Homer's spirit and thirty-eight thousand Dodger hearts in the third with four more, sending him in to an early shower and then pounding his successor on the mound. Everyone on the Yankee side but Joe hit safely, even the pitcher banging the ball into unoccupied territory. Joe Nugent fielded his position acceptably, but at the plate he was self-conscious and unhappy over his boner of the previous day. The Dodgers didn't permit him to forget it, either.

By the last inning a procession of Brooklyn

pitchers had taken the mound, been promptly shelled off, and trudged away to the showers. The score mounted. It was not a contest, it was a walk-over, and the Dodgers accepted the shellacking as part of the game, secure in the knowledge they still possessed an edge in victories.

Spike sat later in the manager's room, clad only in his dirty wet shirt. The reporters stood about him, pencils and paper in their hands. As usual, he was reluctant to make predictions, nor did he wish to name his starting pitcher for the next day.

"Don't know. Can't say, Phil. I'll wait till to-morrow and see."

"Will you use Nugent again in the Series, Spike?"

"Depends. Maybe. Maybe not. If it lasts and he gets rested, I might."

"One game a week, one game a week, that's all old Showboat has left in him," said a scornful voice at the outer edge of the circle.

Spike glanced up from his chair and came in-stantly to the defense of his pitcher. "Let me tell you, he's one fine pitcher in any league if he has a little rest between assignments. After all, he's push-ing forty. Sam Jackson, the Yankee coach, said he was throwing four different kinds of curves yester-day; he was, too. Throwing them from a lot of dif-ferent angles . . ."

"What about his boy, Spike? He did better out there today, didn't he? How about him? How's he shape up to you?"

"Well, a kid like that's on a terrible spot. Shucks, I'd rather not be quoted, boys." He grinned at them. "And look, you guys, don't put that in the papers, either, that's worse'n if I said nothing at all. I know you fellers."

There was a silence. The reporters were finding the Dodger manager tough going. As usual, the beaten skipper hasn't a lot to say. Outside in the big dressing room the players were hustling into their clothes, anxious to get away and leave as soon as possible, to forget the whole horrible afternoon. Someone in the circle about Spike made a last attempt at an angle.

"Well, tomorrow is another day." There was a note of hope in his voice that Spike would pick it up.

Casey broke in sagely. "Tomorrow is the *big* day. Win that one, boy, and they can't catch you. You're in."

"Yep." He rose and pulled off his shirt. When he stood you noticed how he was taped from here to there, to build up and protect his feet, ankles, and legs. He started to yank the tape off. "Yep, tomorrow's the big one, all right. Hey, Casey-boy, you said that, not me. Don't quote me on that either, kid."

The gang laughed and broke up. One or two of them went toward the large room where the players were combing their hair, tying neckties, taking their valuables from old Chiselbeak. Raz sat on the bench before his locker. Since he had been only a spectator that afternoon, he was comparatively fresh.

Some reporter dropped the usual question about his boy, about the boner of the previous day. Raz looked up quickly.

"Aw, that can happen to anyone. Tough it had to happen to the kid in the Series, that's all. Ya don't like to have eighty thousand people see you fall on your face. Well, that's baseball. Shoot, I remember three-four years ago we was behind by two games toward the end of the season. No, yes, two games it was, going into Philadelphia. Spike, he called a last-minute meeting in the clubhouse and gave us a pep talk. Read the riot act, he did. Told us all not to take the Phils lightly just because they was in seventh place, warned us to watch out for 'em, said we'd better keep our eyes open alla time . . ."

"Well, sir—" Raz warmed to his subject as the audience grew. The old Showboat was always good for a gag, and the knot of reporters around his bench increased, men leaning over each other's shoulders, peering down, straining to get Raz's words. "Well, sir, we fell behind four-three. Important game, too, good one to win. Then in a late inning one of our boys hit safely, stole second, and was sacrificed to third in a close play. There was a kind of rhubarb round the bag like that yesterday, and guess what happened. You're right! Ed Myers on third pulled the hidden ball trick and tagged the runner out at third."

Raz's audience laughed obediently at the story. The big chap looked up at them. He hadn't finished. There was a glint in his eyes and a grin on his face.

"The runner? Spike Russell. Oh, sure, we lost the game."

The gang laughed heartily over the anecdote, although they were really laughing as much at old Razzle and his apparent delight in the incident as the story itself.

Then the outside door suddenly burst open. Sandy Dockler of the *Times* stood there, looking around, peering through his glasses. He had been hustling, his face was red and he was panting.

"Hey, you guys," he called across to the knot around the old Showboat. "Hey, guys! Newman's canned young Nugent. He's going with Burwell Kent at second base tomorrow."

CHAPTER FIFTEEN

Raz NUGENT spent some time late that afternoon reflecting upon his son's misfortune. He had
seen plenty of youngsters come up in his time, had
seen many lose out in one short series or even a
single game, watched them go to pieces and blow
their chances in baseball. It could, he knew, happen to the boy. This was something that might even
wreck him for good. But what to do? Raz understood that as a father he had nothing to say to the
youngster. As an old-timer, however, as a veteran
player who had observed them come and go for
years, he might just possibly make the boy listen.
Anyhow, he felt he ought to give it a try.

Unlike some of the Yankee players who were
married and lived with their families in apartments
around the metropolitan area, Joe Nugent stayed

with two other bachelors on the team in a three-room suite in a midtown hotel. That evening Razzle came down the long hallway searching for the numbers on the door. 1403 to 1406. This must be it!

Raz knew baseball. And the rules of the game, written and unwritten. He realized he risked a call from the Commissioner if his visit were discovered. He didn't care, for he felt he had to come, he had to see the boy. So he knocked on the door rather gently. There was no answer. He waited a while and then knocked again, more sharply. Inside someone stirred, a door banged shut in the wind, and a voice answered in a dismal tone, "Yeah."

The door opened to his touch and he entered to find himself in the living room of a suite. Chairs were pushed back from a table in the middle, on which were empty glasses and beer bottles. By the door to one of the bedrooms stood the boy, no cordial expression on his face when he saw the visitor.

"Oh," he said, "I figgered you was Room Service come to clean up."

"Mind if I come in? Just thought I'd drop around a minute or two and talk things over with you. Guess you're pretty low right now, hey boy?" Razzle walked slowly over and sat down in an easy chair without being asked. He didn't expect a cordial invitation and he got none.

He glanced around. Has the boy, he wondered, been drinking? Was he trying to forget in liquor his failure and his subsequent demotion from the team? The old Showboat remembered only too clearly the grim nights in his own past when he had taken the easy way out. The time he roughed up Roy Tucker's room in the Schenley in Pittsburgh and a fine of five hundred dollars had been slapped on him. That important contest in Sioux City when he had loosened up a bit too much the previous night and been called upon to take the mound the next day in a condition when he couldn't see the plate.

The boy, watching him at ease in the big chair, shrugged his shoulders slightly and sank on a hard seat. His head went down, he clasped his hands, staring at the carpet. Raz knew exactly how he felt. In fact nobody in baseball understood better than Raz himself just what it was like to fall flat on your face out there before eighty thousand fans. That is the time when words don't help, when the only thing that helps is to put it completely out of your mind, to forget it. To say, Oh, well, tomorrow's another day.

Razzle glanced over at the beer bottles on the

table again, and then looked closely at the despondent youngster. He was trying hard to figure out whether the kid had been drinking.

"You feel mighty darn low about things, don't you, hey, Joe?"

No response. Not even a nod of the head. Naturally Raz had anticipated hard going after their last meeting, but this was really tough. He wiped his forehead, wondering what to say next. It was sure hard going.

"Son, see here. I felt bad yesterday. I sure did feel for you. I've been there. I know how it hurts. Only don't take on, boy. You'll snap out of it.

"Snap out of it!" There was disgust in his voice. "Snap out of it! Watching from the bench while Kent plays second base. Fat chance . . ."

"Yes, I know and all that, but baseball's a funny game. You've come fast since last July, and you've had the pressure on you something terrible this week. All these build-ups and interviews make it tough for a guy, above all in a Series, believe me. Better guys than you have stumbled in the Series. You've had a big load to carry, son. I saw Marty McDonald of the Cards when he came up in his freshman year. Why, he had everything. Led the National League in batting and was the best-fielding third baseman in the circuit. What happened?

He got the Series jitters, tossed the ball all over the lot, and finished with three scratch singles in a dozen times at bat. That's baseball for . . ."

"I ain't Marty McDonald. I'm Joe Nugent." He rose from his chair and went to the window, looking down without seeing the traffic far below.

"You mustn't take on like this, boy. Mustn't let it get you down. You aren't through, no sir; no siree, you ain't. You was just a little tight, a mite nervous, that's all, and naturally, too, your first Series. Wait and see. You'll get plenty of action in this-here thing yet, plenty of it . . ."

The boy broke in. "Aw, the hell I will!"

"No, I believe you will, I really do. Honest, I'm not just saying that. Look, Joe, you're a better second baseman than Burwell Kent the best day he ever lived." He leaned across to where the boy now sat slumped in the chair and put one hand on his knee. "Ya believe me, son, believe me, don't ya? Not just because you're my boy, either. I mean it. I really do."

Still he said nothing, did nothing, just sat staring at the floor. Razzle saw he wasn't getting very far. He changed signals.

"Look here now. It's seven-thirty. Had anything to eat?"

"Eat? Naw, and what's more I don't want anything either. Not now."

"But you gotta eat, you must eat something, you can't go without your dinner. Come on. What say you an' me go out and chow. I know a nice, quiet little place over here on Seventh Avenue where they sure set you up a steak."

"No thanks."

"Look, son." Raz rose and put his arm around the shoulder of the dejected boy. "I know what you're going through right now. Believe me, I sure do. I've been there, son, more times than once, too."

The boy brushed him off. He turned, twisted in his chair, withdrew his shoulder from the grip of his father's arm, shook off that friendly hand.

I'm not going out with you. I didn't ask you to come here. I don't want you. I never trusted you. I don't now. Get out."

"Aw, Joe, c'mon . . ."

"Not after what you've done to me and to Ma, too. Guess I'll never forget the way I felt the last time you came through town when I was a shaver, how you promised me a bat and a glove, a real Louisville slugger you said you'd send. A guy that breaks his promise to a kid . . ."

Razzle rose, astonishment on his face. His mouth opened. "Hey, look . . ."

"That's the way it always was. You let me down when I was nine years old. You let my ma down too. Why the hell should I trust you now? Get out! Get out, hear me? Leave me alone, I wanna be alone."

Raz Nugent stood motionless and silent. Things began to clear up for him, things such as the boy's hard hatred, his brutal action on the diamond at Kansas City before the packed stands. He spoke quietly. "So you never got that Louisville slugger I sent ya?"

"Got it! 'Course I never got it. You never sent it. Bet I went down to the post office a dozen times the week after you left town. I pestered that poor old postmistress all day long. Why, I even . . ."

"You never got that Louisville slugger?" repeated Razzle, solemnly.

"No! I told you no, I never did. You didn't send it, that's why."

"I sent it all right," said Raz simply. "I didn't forget ya. I sent it by express."

The boy looked up quickly at his father. "By express!" He was startled. "By express?"

"Sure. You don't send baseball bats by mail, you send them by express. I sent it like I said I would. It was your mother, son, the whole thing was your ma. She kicked me out. We'd had a big blow-up that day and she threw me out, said she wanted no more of me nor my money, either. Mind you, I don't blame her in a way. She hated me. She hated me and she hated baseball for what she felt it had done to me, and she was fixed on one thing—not to have you play ball, too. That was her aim, to keep you from going into pro ball. She got the bat and the glove, too. Chucked 'em away, most likely."

For the first time the boy listened. Now for the first time his tension seemed to ease, and for the first time that long day he was thinking about someone else. He was getting another viewpoint, a new angle on the family troubles, of which, he began to realize, he had heard only one side.

Razzle went on. "Now look, son, that's all over. That's past, that's done with. What's happened has happened. It's you who're important, not to let you ruin your future, to keep you on the track here and now. Boy, you've got it, you have a long time ahead, a long while in baseball, a great big future. You're coming up, not going down like me."

Joe softened. He felt his father as a human being for the first time. The old man was no longer just a miserable heel who had left his mother stranded, but a ballplayer like himself. Like him, yet not like him, for he was a man who had been great once and was on the way out. Tired lines about the eyes and mouth told the story, and the waist. It was not thick and flabby but it was not the waist of twenty-one, either.

To his surprise Joe heard himself say hastily, "Why, say now, I couldn't see anything looked that way the other day. Specially that fast ball of yours. You had a hop on your fast one all right. Seems to me you've got everything you ever had."

"For one game, sure. But I'm through. This is my last crack in the majors. I know it. Spike Russell knows it, too. No use kidding yourself, I'm over the dam. At forty you can't pitch winning ball in the majors or the minors, either. But not you. You'll be up here a long, long time, when the boys have forgotten you're the son of that crazy Raz Nugent. . . ."

"Aw shoot, Pa, that ain't so. You've got a lot ahead yet. . . ."

"You'll be Nugent, the only Nugent, the star of the Yanks. And what's more, you mark my words, you'll make some of these guys, these dopey sports-writers who've been on your neck all week, you'll make them eat the things they been sayin' 'bout you."

The boy started to protest. He opened his mouth. You could see plainly where the two teeth were missing in the front of his jaw, the gap where Burwell Kent had smacked him. Raz kept after him.

"Let's you and your old man go out and have a little grub together. We'll go to this little place where no one will see us. Those sportswriters, those buzzards, they got eyes in the back of their heads. You'll feel better soon's you got something in your . . . in your . . ." He hesitated. Somehow he didn't want to use that word, the word his son had used about him in contempt. ". . . In your stomach, hey, kid? I know you will. What about it? How's about it?"

The boy rose. Razzle thought he had won; he was certain he had succeeded. Instead, Joe Nugent shook his head. "No thanks. I got a headache. I'd rather not eat a thing right now. Thanks just the same, Pa, but I'm not for no food." He walked over to one of the doors, opened it, and disappeared into the bedroom within. The door closed.

Raz stepped to the window, shaking his head. Your son, your own flesh and blood in trouble, going through the very same things you had gone through, and there you are, useless. Useless and unable to help.

There was a brisk knock on the door. An efficient lad in a white jacket with a napkin over one arm stood there. "Someone call Room Service to clean up here, sir? You want me to take these things away?"

"Sure, sure, boy. Come on in, clean up this mess."

The boy stood in the doorway, staring at him. "Pardon me, sir, but you're Raz Nugent, aren't you?" He was whipping a pad from his pocket. "I wonder if you'd mind giving me your signature?"

Razzle grinned. "Why, of course, son, with pleasure." He wrote his name on the pad.

"Hope you don't mind my bothering you, Mr. Nugent?"

"Listen, young fella." Raz handed back the pad and pencil. "When folks stop bothering old Raz, he stops eating." There was a grimness in the remark which struck him. That moment isn't too far ahead, either. "There you are. Say, you're quite a baseball fan, aren't you?"

"Yes, sir, I've had all the boys' signatures. Mr. Kent and Mr. Stein and Mr. White and the others."

A thought suddenly came to Raz. He lowered his voice and stepped over toward the waiter. "Are you the man attached to this suite?"

"Yes, sir. I'm Room Service on duty on this floor."

"Did you happen to bring up this order to these gentlemen?"

"Yes, I did, sir."

"Tell me, can you, who was here. D'you recall?"

"Why, yes. There was Mr. Stein and Mr. White

and one or two other boys. I just didn't notice especially."

"I see." Razzle's voice dropped. "Was they all drinking beer?"

"Yes, sir, I believe they all ordered beer. Except one man, one newspaper fella; he had a whisky sour."

"Would you happen to remember if my boy was having beer?"

"No, sir, he wasn't drinking a thing. They tried hard to get him to have a beer or whisky or something to cheer him up. He was sure awful low. But he just wouldn't touch a thing. Oh, he was really down, Mr. Nugent was. Sat there in that chair with his head in his hands, not saying a word."

"I see. Thanks very much."

"Not at all," replied the waiter, loading the empty bottles and the glasses on his tray.

Raz walked across to the door of the bedroom. He knocked softly.

"Anything I can do for you, Joe, you know where to find me."

There was no sound, no answer. He waited a minute, then he turned and walked past the waiter into the hall.

CHAPTER SIXTEEN

THE next day Bones Hathaway was magnificent. He had everything, fast ball, flashing curve, change of pace, and beautiful control. He toyed with the Yankee sluggers; he was ahead of them all the way through, teasing them with his change-up and keeping their hits well scattered. It was perhaps the best-pitched game of the Series so far.

Burwell Kent fielded well and was an acceptable second baseman, but at the plate he went four for nothing, doing not as well as Joe Nugent. When he stepped in with two out and the bases full in the eighth, the stands wondered whether Newman would insert Joe as a pinch hitter, for Kent had shown nothing all afternoon and had even failed to get the ball out of the infield. But the Yankee manager decided to stay with his line-up, and Kent went down swinging on the fourth pitch.

That night the Dodgers went to bed leading three games to one. Everyone who had felt certain that at last the Yankees had found themselves, and would murder the National Leaguers, changed completely around. It was, to be sure, unbelievable that the famous conquerors of the American League couldn't do better than win one game in four against the Bums. But that's how it was. Now the odds shifted to favor the Dodgers, and so did the experts. After all, the Brooks had a commanding lead and needed only one more victory to take the Series.

Then came a break for the victors, the kind of a break that somehow always seems to favor the winning team. It rained hard all day Sunday, and although it cleared up late Monday morning and the field had been protected by a tarpaulin, the turf was soggy underfoot and as a consequence the next contest was postponed until Tuesday. This, of course, meant two days' extra rest for the over-worked Brooklyn pitching staff. As everyone agreed, they could all use those extra days of leisure. It was hard to see any possible outcome but a triumph for the Dodgers.

So sportswriters dug into the record books to discover when the Dodgers had ever come so close before to winning a World Series. They wrote their leads (which of course featured the Dodger victory) early that morning, so as to be ready to flash them to the paper when necessary. By now the Yankees' handicap seemed so overwhelming the only question was when the Brooks would win.

Newman went with Harry Swift, a southpaw, that afternoon. Swift was one of his best pitchers, a man who had won eighteen games and been an important factor in the drive for the pennant. But the Dodgers figured to take him as they had the other Yankee hurlers. They were loose and confident. Spike Russell had his club in hand, and with their ace McCaffrey on the mound, the Brooks took an early lead and maintained it through the game.

High in the press box, Casey was figuring as the last innings came around. He murmured to himself. "Three innings, nine outs to go! The Yanks better move, and fast, too. There! A routine catch. He can't miss, an easy one. Kent hasn't made a hit yet, has he? Newman should have tried young Joe Nugent again today."

"Aw, yer grandmother's doilies," said Sandy, next

to him. "Why'n you tell that to Newman before the game? He'd have thanked you. Maybe."

"Why'n you get a job managing the Yanks?" growled Casey. "At that, you'd do better'n Newman. Score's six to four and only eight outs to go. You can't beat it. I bet you could have got fifty to one in Wall Street last week that the Dodgers wouldn't win but a single game."

It was the eighth, and the Yankees were still two runs behind, with three needed to win. Actually Newman found himself obliged to use Joe that inning. Roy Tucker singled and, going into second with his usual dash, ripped a piece of Kent's thigh in trying to break up a double-play ball. The Yankee infielder had to be assisted off the diamond, and young Joe took over at second base.

Elmer went into the box in the ninth, superbly confident. The score still remained 6 to 4, in favor of the Dodgers. Out in deep right, the Dodger bull pen, which had been up and down from the start, began to work automatically. The first Yankee batter hit a smart grounder almost over second base, but as usual Spike was there waiting for it, scooped it up, and shot it over to first. Now they were only two put-outs from victory.

The next man drove a liner to right which fell in for a single. At this, activity in the Dodger bull pen

became much less automatic. Old Raz, watching
the diamond over his right shoulder, threw in his
pitches with more vehemence.

Then Newman put in Jerry Sands, the Yankee
slugger, to pinch-hit for the pitcher. Elmer went
to work on him with extreme care, perhaps a bit too
carefully. At the full count Sands caught one of his
slants and powdered it. Raz stood in the bull pen,
legs apart, hands on his hips, watching Highpockets
chase that clout to the fence. He turned and went
to work in earnest.

The man on first had scored, making it 6 to 5, and
Jerry Sands ended on second base. Spike came
toward the mound in that tremendous din from the
stands, for now things were happening. At last the
Yankees were unleashing their power, too late perhaps, but threatening nevertheless. The Dodger
manager signaled to the bull pen, and Raz, after
burning in several more pitches, turned and came
across the field. There was confidence and assurance in his gait and bearing. He crossed the
diamond and took the ball from the skipper in that
tremendous roar, completely unconcerned, seem-
ingly unaware of the tenseness of the moment, loose
and easy. If he felt what hung on every pitch, he
didn't show it. It might have been an early-season
game against the Phils. Even Joe on the opposing

bench had to admire his coolness as he stood there, apparently untouched by the crazy madness around.

The batter was the Yanks' first baseman, big Tracy Jones, a name batter who never went for bad pitches, and Razzle worked on him with great deliberation and caution. Tracy was known as a man who crowded the plate, something that Raz invariably resented. He wanted his own share of the platter, so he threw the first pitch close and inside. The man backed hastily away.

Ball one!

Raz then fed him a change-up which Tracy swung on and missed. Strike one! The tension grew. Now the entire Yankee dugout was on the steps calling, appealing to their teammate to hit, to keep the rally alive. The batter fouled off a couple of pitches and it was two strikes and a ball. Razzle could be only four pitches from victory.

The Showboat wasted the next one, hoping against hope that the batter would bite. He didn't, so the count was two and two. Raz was tossing down-breaking stuff, hoping if possible to keep the ball on the ground so his infield could prevent the runner on second base from advancing. This was what happened. The batter hit a hopping slow roller right through the box.

Raz stabbed, missed it, and saw Spike going

over, covering up the ground, taking it in his stride. The runner was well on his way to third by this time, but they could afford to ignore him and nab the slow man at first, which they did easily. Now the Brooks were but a single out from the title.

There was a delay in the Yankee dugout. Joe Nugent was the next batter, and he had gone hitless all through the Series save for his clout in the second game. So everyone gaped, expecting that as he wasn't in the circle ready for his raps Newman planned to put in a pinch hitter. However, the Yankee manager had no more pinch hitters worth sending in, and there was little choice save to go along with his rookie infielder. The delay was caused by the whispered instructions he was giving to the boy on the steps of the dugout. You could see the white-haired man leaning over him, and the boy nodding, impatient to get out there and swing. With quick steps he came to the plate.

On the mound Raz stood watching, hands on his hips. Now the stands were up, everyone on edge for this duel between the two Nugents. Back there in that suite on the fourteenth floor Joe had been his boy, his only son, and Razzle had been trying to help. Out there in the late afternoon with the shadows bisecting the diamond, the youngster in the gray Yankee suit was an enemy to be cut down without the slightest compunction.

This Joe realized perfectly well as he stepped into the batter's box. He knew that all the craft, all the guile and cunning, all the skill and speed his father owned would be brought to bear against him.

"Strike one!" A roar went up from the whole ball park as the Showboat went ahead of the batter when the boy missed one of his slants by a foot. A man on third, the score 6-5, and the Dodgers but a single put-out from victory. Read it the other way around—the Yankees only one put-out from a stunning and unexpected defeat.

The boy stepped back from the box, knocking the dirt out of his spikes. Now the entire crowd was in an uproar, a noise that was continuous, that grew in volume and intensity as Raz toed the mound and stood watching for the signals from Jocko Klein, a roar that increased as he pulled back his big frame, lifted his leg, and went into his motion.

"Strike two!"

The Yankee coach and the runner in the gray uniform dancing along the base path by third and the whole club on the steps of the dugout shouting encouragement to Joe. While from the other side, the bench jockeys yelled through cupped hands and asked questions about his dentist. He heard neither:

indeed in that noise and confusion little could be distinguished a few feet away. He was concentrating on one thing—the ball in his father's hands. Again he stepped out of the box, leaned over, wiped dirt on his sweating hands and over the handle of his bat. He set himself.

It was low and outside, plainly a wasted ball beyond the strike zone. He sighed with relief, a deep, hearty sigh at his escape. Then a strange thing happened, something typical of the old Showboat. The ball in his glove, he stalked cockily toward the plate, and when about halfway and within hearing distance through the din he called out, "Joseph, me lad, this is it!" Then he turned and went back to the mound.

Only Joe and Jocko Klein behind the plate heard it. They both understood immediately, for they both knew the old Showboat. Big Raz in his last moments in baseball intended to leave in a blaze of glory by striking out his son with the tying run on third.

The boy realized his father would use his best pitch, his fast ball, to mow him down, and then would step off the mound in an atmosphere of glory as he went down swinging. So he set himself, dug his spikes into the dirt beside the plate, and waited, watching intently.

It was indeed a fast ball, just under his waist. Joe was ready. He didn't merely meet it, he creamed it, he tattooed it with all he had, with everything he possessed in his wiry shoulders. He hit it, hit it hard, hit it over the moon, over the low barrier into the scrambling, jumping crowd, into the bleachers in deep right center. It was a homer. It was two runs. It was the ball game.

CHAPTER SEVENTEEN

HIGH, high above the stands, up against the white clouds, way above the clamoring thousands below, the press box was alive at last. Every sportswriter had a gleam in his eyes as he hammered away at the copy in his machine. This was something worth while; this was it, this was the real stuff. The World Series, which had begun as the dullest in history, had suddenly caught fire. Up and down the long rows of the working press you heard no casual hum of conversation. The lines of reporters bent to work. It was the sixth game, and Homer Slawson, the Dodger pitcher, had fallen to pieces in the third inning. The Yanks were having a field day and a run-fest.

What makes a top-class pitcher have it all season and then lose his touch? No one has yet figured that

out. Today, as in the third contest, Homer was proving a soft touch for the Yankees. As Casey remarked
curtly while changing paper in his portable typewriter, Homer wasn't throwing hard enough to
break a windowpane.

So the press box was humming with the rat-tat-
tat of the typewriters mingled with the rapid fire
of the telegraphers' keys beside them. This was exciting, something to write about at last. This was
the old Yankees again, Murderers' Row in action,
tying up the Series and making a real thriller out
of the seventh and last battle the next afternoon.
Now the reporters dug their teeth in, and the radio
men in their booths had something to describe
which required no synthetic enthusiasm.

The sensation of the afternoon was young Joe
Nugent. At last he was proving to the National
Leaguers why he was regarded as the best second
baseman in the junior circuit. He started the fire-
works in the third by banging one of Homer's slants
almost out to the Yankee bull pen in deep left
center. He cut off a promising Dodger rally in the
next inning with three aboard when he grabbed
Spike Russell's red-hot liner just over second base
and turned it into an easy double play. When he
came up in the fifth, Spike moved his outfield well
around toward right, and Joe promptly smacked a

slow, lazy liner just over third base, inside the foul line. Rounding first, he took off like a speedboat while the Dodger outfielder stood holding the ball a second before throwing. By the time he had recovered and shot it to second, Joe was sliding in triumphantly under Spike's glove.

In the sixth, Joe handled every chance in the field himself: throwing out Bob Russell in a sparkling play near first; getting the next man, a pinch hitter for Homer, on a pop-up behind second; and then going back to snare Zimmerman's Texas leaguer in short right field. All the while Jake Stein, the Yankee right-hander, had the Dodgers under control. He was never in trouble from the start.

In the last of the sixth, there was a volley of cheers as Joe stepped to the plate. Back on the Dodger bench, old Razzle, his arms folded, chewed violently as he watched his boy come in for his raps. He yanked at his cap when the youngster hit safely again, whistling a single over second this time, rounding first, and then retreating cautiously to the bag. On the first pitch, however, Joe was off to second. The throw was high and he slid in safely.

Casey, a National Leaguer from way back, growled. "Aw," he muttered, "he wouldn't have been doing that if Jocko Klein's shoulder was right."

"Yeah," said the reporter next to him in the press

box, "except that he's been doing that on every catcher in the American League since the tenth of August!"

Forty minutes later, Spencer Newman sat in the manager's room with a cigar in his mouth, grinning broadly. Stripped to the waist, he leaned back in his chair, talking amiably to Casey, for no Pinkerton man barred reporters from the room this afternoon.

"Yessir, I've been telling you boys that kid had the stuff. Now he's shown everyone; well, he's been like that for us since early August. See why we were high on him, Casey? Believe me, he's got plenty of heart, too. He showed you folks his stuff out there today after a pretty dismal start. Thing about that boy is, he was playing his first Series under pressure, and you guys just naturally made it tough for him . . ."

Casey broke in. "We guys! What do you mean, we guys! We didn't fumble those balls out there . . ."

"Nope, but you sure helped him to do it, building him up the way you did. If he was Ruth and Cobb and DiMaggio rolled into one and multiplied by ten, he couldn't have lived up to that guff you wrote, you an' Dockler an' . . ."

"For my book he's mighty near living up to that right now."

"Say, that diving catch Joe made in the fourth with three on, that stab which set up the double-play ball . . ." One of the coaches entered and ripped off his shirt. "Why, that was one of the greatest stops I've ever seen in a World Series, and I've seen plenty. Those guys were all set to go for Stein, but Joe just smothered them. He's really got it, that kid. Some players would have quit after the bust he made of the first few games. . . ."

"You're right, Sam," said Newman. "You're dead right there. A lot of kids I know would have cracked wide open after those first three-four games. Not Joe. That makes me think, too, I have a message for him."

He went to the door of his room and called out. "Hey, Joe! You know they expect you over at NBC, don't ya? Some fella called and left word, said you was to be sure and show at Studio Eight E at five-thirty. Asked should he come in a car and fetch you? No, I said, you was reliable. So be sure and get there at five-thirty. Those broadcasting people want you on time, you know, they don't ever wait. . . ."

CHAPTER EIGHTEEN

Both bull pens went into action in earnest from the very first pitch that next afternoon. In fact, every hurler on both sides who could walk and throw was in the two respective bull pens getting ready as the game began. They knew they were likely to be called on at any moment. This last game of the World Series was in New York, so the Dodgers batted first. Fuller went for the Yankees. Bones Hathaway, who had won the fourth game, was throwing for the Brooks. Each team seemed to have its batting cap on, and the Yanks especially were hitting hard from the start.

But good fielding kept anyone from the bases until the last of the third, when Tracy Jones, the first batter, drove a deep high one between right and center field. By the time the ball was relayed to the infield, Jones was panting on second base. Spike Russell came anxiously toward the box. Taking no chances, he was determined to use every single man in the bull pen to stop the Yankee sluggers. He glanced at the far corner where four or five pitchers were throwing vigorously. Ricketts? No, he relieved yesterday. Dickinson? No, they've been murdering lefties. That leaves Razzle, Robbie, and Stone. Thus far Raz has been the most effective of the lot.

So he signaled from the mound as he had done so often that summer, not with his arms extended in a circle as formerly, but holding up his right hand for his number-one reliever. The Showboat came across the field to an accompaniment of delighted yells from the Brooklyn fans. Spike and Jocko Klein and Bob Russell were grouped about the mound, watching him approach. Half a dozen photographers were waiting also, and several were standing or kneeling near the plate where Joe Nugent was ready to step in for his raps.

"Gosh! This-here's a tough setup for the old guy to walk into, having to throw against his own boy. Someone ought to say something, loosen him up, sort of."

"Something like what?" asked Jocko.

"Oh, anything, anything at all," said Spike, "just

to take the pressure off him when he sees the boy at the plate. You think of something. He likes you, you'll help him."

Jocko shook his head. At the moment he felt unable to come up with any bright remark. Man on second, nobody out, last game of the Series, and Joe Nugent, the boy who had found his eye again and was clouting every pitcher all over the lot, at bat.

"*I* think of something! Not me," said Jocko. "Nuts, I can't think of anything. You think of something, you're the manager."

Spike took a couple of steps out to meet the big fellow who came toward him with quick, confident movements. You might almost imagine he came in there eagerly, that he looked forward to the tenseness and tightness of it, the enemy player on second, the yelling and clap-clapping of the Yankee fans in the grandstand. In fact it seemed as if the situation appealed to his competitive spirit. Spike neared him, slapping his hands together a couple of times. "O.K., Razzle, old-timer. You did it before, you can do it now, Raz-old-kid-old-boy."

Raz paid not the slightest attention. He almost appeared not to have heard his boss speak. He was grim and set. "Gimme that ball, Skipper, lemme have that-there ball." Even from the stands it was plain enough that the old Showboat was less nervous then than any other man on the diamond.

Spike nodded and tossed the ball over. He felt happy he had chosen Razzle, for he realized what was going on in the big fellow's heart and mind. Evidently he was anxious to make up for that terrible error of the fifth game when, facing his son with the Series as good as won, he had showboated and kicked it out of the window.

Razzle stepped to the mound, all business as he threw in his warm-ups, surveying the boy at the platter as calmly and impersonally as if this were an exhibition game in Valdosta, Georgia, in spring, and the kid was merely another rookie up for a try-out from a Yankee farm club. In fact there was a purposeful look in the way the old-timer went to work that Spike had seldom seen him display before. There was no showmanship whatever, no playing to the crowd now, no stunts of any kind. Only one thing—a ruthless concentration on the task before him.

Raz seemed somehow to tower above the youngster at the plate, nodding ever so slightly at Jocko, who squatted and gave him the sign. With the runner dancing wildly off second, and the row of photographers on their haunches ready to catch the first run of the game, and the Yankee coaches shrieking through cupped hands to rattle him, and the stands on their feet yelling, too, Raz bent over. He was the old master and for once the youngster at the plate was a fumbling beginner.

The first ball was a strike which the boy took as the Brooklyn fans rose, hysterically yelling. Like Spike Russell they were sure the old Showboat would pull them through. The next was a hook that Joe fouled off vainly. Then followed a teaser, low and inside, which he took. Finally Razzle came in with his fast ball, close, so close you could feel the batter's indecision, his uncertainty whether to swing or not.

The hand of the umpire went out to his right, his body twisted. Joe had been cut down on four straight pitches.

The following hitter popped weakly in front of the plate. Jocko, running out, smothered the ball as the runner on second backtracked and retreated hastily to the bag. Now there were two down. The next man grounded to Spike Russell, who tossed in plenty of time to Zimmerman on first, leaving the Yankee runner stranded. The photographers turned and walked back to the stands, while Raz stepped majestically from the box, the Brooklyn crowd roaring with joy. He chucked his glove over the base line in that familiar gesture of pride and assurance. The yowling from the stands increased; here was the old Showboat.

"Hey there, Showboat."

"Oh, you Showboat."

"Attaboy, Razzle!"

He straightened up, turned toward the Dodger bench, and walked by Joe, who was on his way out to the field, without a word, tipping his cap ever so slightly to the stands as they passed.

Neither team scored in the fourth or fifth. It was plain that Raz had his stuff. In the sixth, the first Yankee batter hit a long fly ball which Roy Tucker in center went after. He drifted gracefully back, turned and waited. As the ball descended he slapped his glove twice, giving it the twosey. One out. Then Tracy Jones, who had been troublesome for Razzle, stepped in. For the first time the big pitcher got behind on a batter. The count went to three and two, and Tracy lined the ball over second for a clean single. Spike, watching anxiously, saw young Joe come to the plate.

Raz wasted a ball and then got a strike, on which Tracy slid into second on Jocko's bad shoulder. A man on second, one down. So, taking no chances, Spike gave Razzle orders to walk the boy and set up the double play. As expected, the following batter bunted to advance both runners.

With amazing agility, Raz pounced on the ball, turned and fired to cut off the advancing Yankee runner. The Dodger third sacker stepped on the bag. Then, seeing young Joe almost at second, he threw to first, hoping for a double play. Joe was running. He tore around second base and high-tailed for third. Although the batter was safe on first, the throw had been accurate and the first base-man, seeing Joe taking liberties on the base paths, gunned the ball back across the diamond. The youngster was a dead duck, out by at least five feet. But instead of coming in conventionally, he slid forward head first in a twisting slide, swerving wide and grabbing the corner of the bag with out-stretched hand. The third baseman swung round to tag him in vain. Joe came in under the tag and was safe on third.

Now there were men on first and third and two out. Raz toed the rubber quickly. He nodded to Jocko, for he wanted to cut the Yankees down and was fearful Spike would decide to replace him on the mound. He took the signal, while Joe with out-stretched arms danced gleefully back and forth on the base path. Then the big fellow whipped in a strike. The batter took the next pitch, which was low and outside. After that things happened so fast that

Casey up in the press box, his head half-buried in his typewriter, had trouble following the ball.

With no windup, Raz shot in his pay-off pitch, his fast ball. The batter swung vainly for the second strike. Instantly Jocko rifled the ball in a split-second play to third, catching Joe in his run-up, five feet from the bag. The pattern on the field instantly changed. Everyone started running, Jocko advancing threateningly toward the Yankee star, the Dodger third sacker feinting with the ball, pretending to throw, Spike rushing over to cover the bag, Bobby Russell camping on second, Paul Roth racing in from deep left field, and the other Yankee runner taking a lead off first, ready to cut for second if the chance presented itself.

Back and forth, back and forth went the ball, back and forth from Jocko to the third baseman and then to Jocko again. They closed in on the trapped runner, nearer, nearer, when with a sudden, amazing burst of speed Joe shouldered his way past the stocky catcher and set sail with all speed for the plate some thirty feet away.

There was a gasp from the big crowd. The third baseman, who had the ball, calmly pegged to Raz, camped and waiting at home. Joe roared in, realized he was out, and took the only and obvious chance. He went in with such force that Razzle, set and ready as he was, sprawled in the dirt behind the platter while Joe tumbled and bounced off on the other side. Raz held on to the ball despite the fearful impact, and even as he crashed to the ground managed to keep one foot on the plate. Half a dozen Dodgers rushed out from the dugout.

They yanked Raz, half dizzy from the collision, to his feet. Supported by his teammates, who were congratulating him, patting him on the back, and dusting him off all at the same time, he turned, amid the cheers and shouts, and started to trudge to the mound, forgetting for the moment that the inning was over. Halfway out he paused and leaned over, for the wind was almost knocked out of him. Then he straightened up, waved a reassuring hand at the manager who was running in, and realizing this was the third out, moved back toward the dugout, chucking his glove over the foul line. The big finger pointed directly toward third. Raz, tipping his cap again very slightly, staggered to the bench and the ministrations of Doc, who waited for him with smelling salts and a dry towel.

The wise guys in the press box watched the bull pen to see whether after that upset Spike would stay with his pitcher or call in another man. There was no evidence of a replacement, however, and Raz stepped out for the seventh apparently as fresh as ever. The seventh went past uneventfully, and the game was still a scoreless tie as the teams entered the eighth. From his spot at short, Spike Russell watched every pitch, anxiously waiting for the first sign of fatigue or weariness on Razzle's part, ready to call in a relief man any moment. But although the big man was sweating freely, he seemed full of confidence and in complete control of his assortment of pitches. He had the Yankee hitters still swinging. Starting as a replacement, he seemed to get better as the game went along.

The hitters paraded to the plate and went down before his craft and cunning. At no time was he really in danger after those tight moments in the sixth, and no Yankee batter got beyond first base. The eighth moved on into the ninth, both teams deadlocked; the tenth came up and still there was no score. So far Razzle had allowed exactly three clean hits. Shadows deepened over the ball park; over the crowd packed up in the stands, standing at the back in the uppermost reaches of the second tier; over the old Showboat in the box. It was the last of the eleventh.

Joe Nugent, waving his club, was up at bat again.

With one man out, Tracy Jones had beaten out a slow roller and reached first. Spike glanced at his hectic bull pen, thinking it was time for a change, and walked across the diamond. Yet he had no feeling of assurance that he was doing the right thing in switching, that a fresh pitcher would be any improvement over Razzle at the moment.

Jocko Klein came out toward the two men beside the mound.

"How ya feeling, Razzle?" asked Spike.

"O.K., Spike. How *you* feeling, kid?"

Tense as the moment was, even the worried manager was forced to grin. "How ya figure this boy, Showboat?"

"Look, Spike," said the big chap, slapping the ball viciously into his glove. "Look, I've gotten him out every time he faced me but once, haven't I? O.K., lemme get him out this time, too."

Spike understood. No one realized better than he that Raz wanted to win this one on his own, that the Showboat was on the rubber for the last time in his career in the majors.

Razzle was firm, set, fixed; he stood astride the rubber as if he owned it, legs apart, sure of himself. Hard to throw out a pitcher feeling that way, a man who had given up three hits in eight innings. Spike turned to the black-haired catcher.

"How's his stuff, Jocko?"

"As good as it was any time in this game! As good

as any time I ever caught him," replied Jocko quickly.

Spike nodded. That settled it. He placed one hand on the big pitcher's right arm.

"I'm riding along with you, Raz."

He turned in the din and trotted back to his spot in the field.

CHAPTER NINETEEN

W HAT'S he think he's doing now?" asked Casey of the reporter sitting next him.

On the diamond below, Spike Russell held up one hand to old Stubblebeard to call time. He ran toward the pitcher's box.

"Say! Must have changed his mind. Guess he's going with a new pitcher."

"No," said Casey, all attention. "He isn't changing pitchers. It's something else. Not now, he isn't."

Razzle, hands on his hips, nodded as Spike rushed past, saying something to him. The manager extended an arm to the Brooklyn dugout, while Raz walked briskly to the plate, patting Jocko Klein, who stood with his head turned toward the bench, on the arm. Apparently, with that speed boy on first the Dodger manager felt it unwise to take any more chances on Jocko's injured shoulder and his consequent uncertain throwing to bases.

Big Mike Todd, the second-string receiver, hurried out of the dugout. He leaned over and buckled on the shin pads, then stepped in to receive Razzle's pitches, while Jocko retired to the dugout with the cheers of the fans in his ears. Mike threw to second, took the ball on the return, and walked out toward Raz, flipping it in his hand. When a few feet away he nodded confidently and tossed it over.

So there they were for the ninth time in the Series, the young Nugent and the old Nugent. Each one respected the other at last, because each one had shown in a crisis what he had inside him. But each was set to do one thing—to pin the other's ears back. Oblivious to the crowd and the tightness of the moment, they glared back and forth, concentrated on the task at hand.

On the mound Raz stood with his legs apart, glancing over toward first, yanking at his cap. His right foot toed the rubber. He reared back and let go. He meant it to be just what it was—a deceptive hook that caught the corner of the plate while the batter remained motionless. Once again he had won the first round; once again he was ahead of the boy. The crowd rose in tribute as Razzle bent over to finger the rosin bag, straightened up, hitched at his pants for the hundredth time that afternoon. All the while the nervous boy beside the plate scuffed the dirt with his spikes, swinging his bat, intent on the ball to come.

Raz snapped it off quickly. This time Joe met it squarely. This was the one he had been waiting for and he hit with all he had, smacked it long, hard, and deep toward right field. The base runner was off, rounding second and charging into third, and Joe had passed first when the first-base umpire waved his hand frantically. The ball was foul by two feet.

Spike ran over, took the new ball thrown in by the catcher, and walked across to Raz.

"Hey, watch it, Showboat! That was too close for comfort. He can powder that ball."

"Don't you worry none," said Raz. "Don't worry none, Spike. I'll get him for you."

Joe walked slowly back to the batter's box and they faced each other again, father and son, each with the Nugent confidence, each with that amazing Nugent ability to come through in the clutch. Razzle came in with a hook, but it was high. The catcher stepped back one pace, poised to throw, but the dancing runner on first, who had made a feint toward second, ducked back onto the bag.

One ball and two strikes. Spike fingered the dirt nervously with the finger tips of his left hand, spitting into his glove. The chatter over the diamond had long since died away; the rival dugouts were silent. Too much was at stake and, besides, both the actors in the drama had now proved themselves. You couldn't upset a Nugent, that was plain enough to everyone. Spike wished you could, wished the youngster still had the Series jitters, watched Raz shake off his catcher, and wondered for the tenth time whether he had been smart to take Jocko Klein away from the plate. Raz depended on Jocko; he never shook him off.

It was the sign for the fast ball, and this time Razzle let go with everything he had. The boy was waiting. He met it with the fat of his bat, and the ball came back like a bullet at Raz, who was way over in his stride and completely off balance. Unable to duck, unable even to throw up his hand in protection, Raz caught the ball squarely on the left side of his forehead. It bounced off, rose high in the air. Hopping around like a pain-crazed elephant, he turned, searching, unable to locate it at first. The whole infield called to him, yelling directions.

"There . . ."

"Above ya . . ."

"Behind, Raz . . . there 'tis!"

It dropped, bouncing along a few yards back of him. He turned, groped, reached for it, and threw mechanically to second base. Too late. Now the door was open, for two runners were aboard with only one man down.

Razzle stood on the mound surrounded by the catcher and the rest of the infield, rubbing that angry-looking lump which was growing every second on his prominent forehead. From his spot astride first base Joe watched. He saw the Brooklyn trainer run out, his little black bag in one hand.

"Nope . . . seems like there's no fracture there . . . on that side." He felt the other side, too. It seemed as if Raz might live.

Spike shook his head mournfully. That's luck for you. Your star pitcher knocked out at a critical point in the game by a lucky shot. He had turned toward the bull pen when someone grabbed him by the arm and spun him round. It was Razzle.

The old Showboat was in agony, sore and weary, but he was determined to finish. He intended to win on his own. No, he wouldn't quit. His sharp tones carried over to the youngster on first. Indeed the whole crowd could see what was going on.

"Here, Spike, doggone it. Gimme that ball. Gimme that ball and I'll getcha out of this, darn quick, too."

Spike hesitated. You make the wrong decision and bang, you're through! Every second-guesser in baseball, every sportswriter and every radio reporter, is laughing at you the next day and telling you what you did wrong. Half the pilots in the minors are watching eagerly to see whether or not you get fired. Shoot, this is tough!

The Dodger bull pen was going all out, each man throwing as if he were on the mound and the contest depended on every pitch he made. No wonder Spike hesitated, glanced at the bull pen, reflecting again that perhaps he had taken Jocko out at the wrong moment. Then he saw Razzle stepping toward the rubber without a word. The big fellow's cap was on the back of his head and the swelling showed, but his lips were set and a determined frown was on his face.

Shaking his head, Spike trotted back to his place at short. After all, the old guy sure has earned his chance to put out the fire. The crowd gave Razzle a tremendous hand, for the bump was plainly visible in the grandstand as he gently fingered his forehead.

Raz glanced at first, then over his shoulder at second. Even in his pain he felt no animosity toward Joe. In fact, he was not thinking about the boy at all just now. He was a money player and this was the moment when a pitcher had to deliver, when a guy showed what was inside him.

Taking the signal, he nodded confidently to the catcher and threw in a quick strike. Once again he was ahead of the hitter. The crowd roared in ecstasy as the hand of the umpire behind the plate went up. Even the men in the bull pen paused momentarily to look over their shoulders and watch the drama on the diamond.

The next ball was high, inside; one and one. Raz started to shake his head impatiently, then stopped quickly as a stab of pain ran through his forehead. For just a second he had forgotten that angry bump. He glanced once more over his shoulder at second base where Spike was dancing behind the runner; then he checked Joe, a very whirling dervish on the base paths, at first. Without any warning he threw in another pitch.

"Ball two!"

The stands groaned, cheered, moaned, yelled, and an uneasy rustle swept over the Dodger bench. Was the old Showboat losing his stuff at last? Had that blow affected his control? Everyone on the field wondered, and all the grandstand managers had him on his way to the showers. But not Spike Russell, who actually made the decisions. Spike and Raz were counting to themselves.

One . . . two . . . three . . . four.

Their synchronization was perfect. Spike broke from his spot in deep short at precisely the same second that Raz, who apparently had been taking the signal from his catcher, turned suddenly and threw to the empty base. The pick-off play, as old as baseball, depends on speed and timing. It was a play that Raz and the young manager had worked and worked upon, had perfected over the years, a play they had used with success all through the season. The Yankees knew this; they should have been ready.

But so perfectly executed was it that Spike, charging in to second two steps ahead of the runner, caught Razzle's accurate throw and slapped it on Tracy Jones just as he slid back in to the bag. The unexpected play at just the right moment, the vital second of the contest, the play to cut off the Yankee rally!

The crowd roared, the shrieks and howls of delight from the Brooklyn fans audible above the groans of the Yankee supporters. The throngs from Brooklyn jeered the disconsolate Yankee runner as he picked himself up, dusted the dirt from his pants, and jogged off on that long, long walk, that stretch from second base to the bench. A play of this sort makes the coach look bad as well as the player. The third-base coach was Spencer Newman himself, who had taken the coaching lines that inning after Razzle's injury when the two Yanks had reached base safely.

Two out and a man on first. Once again Raz had things under control; once more the old Showboat had seen defeat facing him and shut the door in its face. As he had done so often during the race for the pennant, he was saving things when the situation looked bleak. A slider or two, a fast ball burned past the hitter, a change-up to fool him, and they would be out of it. Razzle would be sitting there in the coolness of the dugout, most likely watching his pinch hitter. For he was due to bat the next inning and he knew this was his last time on the mound.

He sent in a low, down-breaking curve, and the batter hit an easy rolling ball toward third, the easiest kind of a chance. The simplest kind of a ball to flub at that particular moment, too. But the Dodger infielder waited for it calmly, scooped the ball up, and threw to first for the last and final out of the inning.

Raz stepped off the rubber, took his glove in his other hand, and started with relief to walk in to the bench. Then he froze. The throw was high, so high that even tall Tommy Zimmerman could hardly reach it, so wild that all he could do was knock it down. Instead of the inning ending, there were now men on first and second, and some big ones coming to the plate, too.

Many pitchers would have been sore and resentful. Some pitchers at that tense moment would have shown it to everyone in the ball park, too. Not Razzle. He had been there, he knew what it felt like to stumble in such a spot, and he took the ball after they had tossed it around the diamond. Then he turned and stepped over toward the dejected third baseman.

"No matter, kid," he called across to him. "No matter, don'tcha worry none. I'll get this man."

Back to the box, still ready to bear down and give everything he had, went the old Showboat. The batter caught his first pitch. It was a long, low single to left center. Raz saw Spike's tremendous leap, and his arm vainly extended to intercept the liner, and Roy Tucker galloping across to cut it off in deep center field. Clearest of all he saw Joe, that antelope, that express train, tearing off from second, rounding third, bearing down toward the plate and victory with every bit of energy in his long legs. Roy could throw as well as hit, and his return to the plate was straight and true, right at the catcher on the first bounce.

But Joe Nugent was faster. He ate up the ground.

With a desperate slide he came in under Todd's mitt just as the ball reached home.

The entire Yankee squad poured out of the dugout. Hands out, they converged upon the dust cloud around the plate. They hauled and yanked Joe roughly to his feet, slapping his back, pulling at his arms, trying vainly to shake his hand.

All the while the old Showboat, a figure of pain, with that enormous swelling plainly visible, stepped off the mound, his distress suddenly showing in defeat. For once Razzle's big chin was down. No one surrounded him. No one tried to grab at his hand, either hand, or reached out to clap him on the back. In sport there is no time for the loser. Only victory counts. Only the winner is important; at least, that's what the record books say.

However, one person had not forgotten him. A lone figure fought, struggled, then broke loose at last from the frantic mob about home plate, and ran across toward Raz. It was Joe Nugent, the sensation of the Series, the youngster who jumped from Savannah to the Yankees in a single season, the Nugent who was on his way up. He ran over toward old Raz, the Nugent on his way down. Disappointed and injured and sore in body and mind, Razzle, the losing pitcher in his last battle on the mound, was walking alone to the dugout and the showers.

Now the boy was at his side. He threw an arm around those sagging shoulders. You could see he meant the gesture, too. Raz turned, saw him, and extended his own arm around the shoulders of his only son.

Then a semicircle of vultures blocked their path. Half a dozen photographers kneeled before them, cameras at their eyes. "Hey, Young Razzle! Hey there, Young Razzle, step over this way, will ya? Over here, please!" shouted one of them, forgetting in the excitement that the boy's name was Joe. Joe turned toward him, grinning. "Take me with my old man, boys. You gotta take me right here with my pa."

That was how they left the field, together—Young Razzle and the old Showboat.